Jus[illegible]ardener

Other books by the same author:

Autobiographical

Growing Up in Wigan 1930–1950

The Eefamy Trilogy of historical novels

Number Eighteen

Blue Sailing

Stranded

The above books are obtainable from
Blenheim Press Ltd
Codicote Innovation Centre
St Albans Road
Codicote
Herts SG4 8WH
01438 820281
www.blenheimpressltd.co.uk

Just a Gardener

F. S. (Joe) Winstanley

Blenheim Press Limited
Codicote

Published in 2009
by
Blenheim Press Ltd
Codicote Innovation Centre
St Albans Road
Codicote
Herts SG4 8WH
www.blenheimpressltd.co.uk

ISBN 978-1-906302-17-7

Typeset by TW Typesetting, Plymouth, Devon

Printed and bound in Great Britain by
CPI Antony Rowe, Chippenham and Eastbourne

Acknowledgements

I was helped by Mr Ravenscroft of Bridgemere Nurseries near Nantwich and Mr Chapman of Follyfield Nurseries at Willaston in The Wirral. Mr Peter Seabrook wrote to recommend a book by Roger Aylett who runs a nursery near St Albans and I did find this book useful.

Doreen Mosedale also deserves my thanks for translating my handwritten manuscript.

Also Rob Mosedale for his computer expertise.

Thanks should also go to my wife, Lorna,
for providing a photograph for the cover
and for her general help and encouragement.

ONE

Major Brassington was doing what he did best: arranging a polo match and going to check on the cricket ground to make sure everything was ready for net practice prior to tomorrow's big game. Major Brassington was in Peshawar, fifty miles from the Khyber Pass, and the area was surrounded by war-like Pathans, but these people were not the Major's concern; they were the concern of His Majesty's Government in London. The year was 1936 and the whole of India was part of Britain's Colonial holdings, and down through the system of government, via the War Office, the Colonial Office, and various high ranking Generals right down to Brigadier Ashton in Peshawar, the main emphasis was on quelling uprisings and ensuring that India – the whole of India – knew its place: it was a British Colony. True, it covered fifty times the area of the United Kingdom and had twenty times the population, but it was British, and Brigadier Ashton and the Green Howards were there to make sure the Indians knew their place.

The only person who was not remotely interested in Government policies or military decisions was Major Brassington. No one quite knew how he had attained the rank of Major, just as no one understood how he managed to hang on to it and not be demoted or even cashiered. As a military man he was quite useless. He was universally disliked by his fellow officers and hated and feared by the NCOs and men. He was sarcastic and irritable, he treated his servants badly and was ruthless to the Indians who looked after the polo and cricket fields. Likewise the Officers' Mess catering staff he ruled with a positively wicked authority, and no one knew quite why his duties were limited to various forms of relaxation and entertainment – he was certainly not suited to these aspects of life, since his own capacity for enjoyment was decidedly stunted. But there it was, and because, within this admittedly limited sphere, he was so good at what he did, no one queried it.

When Brigadier Ashton first assumed command of the Peshawar and Rawalpindi area he called a meeting of all his officers and held a dinner at Peshawar. Over one hundred sat down to a palatial meal: the finest wines were served with each course. To salute the fact that most of those present were English, the meal ended with a roly-poly suet pudding and then Cheddar and Stilton cheeses and a really rich port wine – this meal was served late in the evening when the temperatures had moderated, but it was still hot and everyone was in full dress uniform. Except of course Major Brassington, who enjoyed every course which they had eaten indoors, but had his, wearing shorts and an open neck shirt, seated on an open balcony with pleasant twilight breezes caressing him.

No one missed him, so no one commented on his absence, he had gambled on that, but early next day he was asked to go to the Brigadier's office at 11 am. He was always up early, so he had breakfast and then walked to the cricket field, where he saw that the nets were already in place, then checked to make sure the pads had been whitened with blanko and that the pitch was suitably mowed and marked out. He went into the pavilion and sorted out his favourite bat. He would be playing in this match, he had arranged it. He handed the bat to one of the attendants and told him to lock it away, and to be there when the match started to give him access to the chosen bat.

Then Major Brassington, immaculately dressed, with his malacca cane under his arm, marched off to meet his Brigadier. He was shown into his superior's office by a Staff Sargeant, stood to attention and saluted as per text book – he loved saluting and even more, he loved to be saluted, it went hard for anyone who failed in this regard. Some subalterns had thrown him up untidy or sloppy salutes upon first acquaintance, and been told exactly how a salute should be given. Sometimes they had been made to repeat the gesture until it was to Major Brassington's satisfaction. The salute, immaculate though it was, was not a source of pleasure to Brigadier Ashton, who had enjoyed too much of the excellent port the night before, not to mention the single malt whiskies. The Major had a habit of stamping his foot as he saluted, the sound of which reverberated around the office, so that the furniture shook and the Brigadier 's head seemed to him to be in danger of falling off.

'Sit down Major – a drink?'

'No I'll just have coffee Sir, if you don't mind – they'll bring it in.'

And they did. The catering staff knew exactly what Major Brassington had to be provided with, and precisely at what time it would be required.

Brigadier Ashton was slightly bemused by the fact that this Major, who was generally held to be of no use to anyone, held sway over at what time and exactly which beverage should be served in his, the Brigadier's office, but he let it pass, his head was not equal to the task, and anyway he needed the coffee. It was a particularly good hearty flavour, he held the cup away from him as if to display his approbation.

'I get it from London, Sir, as beans,' said Major Brassington. 'We grind it here. It goes off, you know, if they send it out already ground.'

The Brigadier grunted. 'Fine occasion last evening, everyone loved it, they say you arranged everything.'

'We can't let the old country down you know Sir – must keep up the standards.'

'We don't eat like that at Rawalpindi, so how do you do it?'

'I have a brother in London and he has contacts in the catering trade – he is an accountant, and he does the books for the Savoy, Simpsons and one or two more, and he keeps me supplied with the best provisons and tips on how to keep standards up.'

'Well it certainly works. Now about this cricket match, how about today, since all the young officers are here?'

'It is arranged, Sir. We are ready, and I have asked all concerned to be at the ground by 12 noon.'

'What about the teams?'

'I have had team sheets prepared and two scorers have the necessary books, pencils etc, and we have a new scoreboard this season. Tea and sandwiches are laid on for the interval between the innings.'

This welter of efficiency was more than the hung-over Brigadier had expected – he quite forgot to ask the virtually unemployed (in military terms) Major what he intended to do to get back into the main-stream of Army life.

Major Brassington finished his coffee, assumed (incorrectly) that the interview was over, stood up stamped, saluted, turned about with thundering feet, making the office and the Brigadier's head rattle, and went off about his business – such as it was.

The cricket match began promptly at 12 noon. Many of the officers' wives attended and scores of Indians surrounded the ground. Major Brassington won the toss and decided to bat first – in both senses of the word. He strode out with a young lieutenant who had played for his College, and second team County Cricket, but this did not register with the Major. He just said quite simply 'I'll face first.' He met the first ball eight or ten feet out of the crease and clubbed it to boundary – he then grunted. Four of the fielders had been placed quite close to the bat by the fielding Captain – they looked to him for guidance – should they move away, a little? No indication was forthcoming. The second ball was short and rising, Brassington swivelled and smashed it past the square leg umpire for another four. He then raised his bat aloft, twirled it round in his hands, grunted and took his stance for the next ball. The nearby fielders did not look to their Captain for permission, they stepped away two or three paces. He missed the next ball: had he hit it, it would have disappeared out of the ground, but he scored off the remaining three balls.

At the end of the over his batting partner came to the middle to offer his congratulations.

'Only way to play – I can't do with this forward defensive prod business. If I can see it, I'll try to hit it.'

The young man was not really built for belligerent cricket but he stroked two or three nice shots and found the Major a cooperative, if noisy, runner of ones and twos. Brassington faced up again and took sixteen off the next over, with the young lieutenant looking on from the other end with an expression which combined admiration with disbelief. The next over, the hitter was out, caught on the boundary, he sportingly shouted to the fielder 'Well caught' and signalled to the next batsman to get a move on. He had scored 34, and they were only three overs into the match. The Major's side were all out for 137 and tea was taken. After half an hour, Brassington gruffly indicated that tea was over. He grabbed a new ball out of the box and strode out to meet the enemy. Sandwiches and teas were hurriedly finished by his team members, whilst the more fortunate spectators had time for extra tea and the opportunity to try out the sponge cakes.

Major Brassington examined the pitch and decided he would bowl first – and from which end – no surprises there. What was surprising – indeed alarming, was the way he bowled. He was a large powerful man in his middle forties, no longer a young man, but he unleashed the ball with a ferocity rarely met with. He more or less strolled up to the wicket to deliver the first ball, and with an action closely resembling a demented wind-mill, he hurled the ball at the unsuspecting recipient, who was usually caught quite unawares, as in this case, and the wickets were flattened.

'Watch him – he's quick' were the completely unnecessary words offered to the incoming batter by his crestfallen colleague. Orthodoxy and the Major were not even close acquaintances, and he continued to bowl in this explosive manner for the next half hour. It was a hot day, he had taken three wickets and he had had enough, so he tossed the ball to a younger man and stood in the slips to get his breath back. From the slips, he needed and used all the breath that was available to him, as he barked out his instructions and kept everyone on their toes. His team won. He walked off the pitch into the pavilion, but made no attempt to join in the match post-mortem which invariably follows any game. He sought out the pavilion attendant, told him to lock up his bat, and to go to his quarters and make sure that a hot bath was ready for him in ten minutes.

At the cricket ground, pleasant conversation carried on for another hour. There were cakes to finish and an endless supply of tea. Sun shades were everywhere and comfortable chairs were spread beneath them. The organiser of all this luxury and comfort was not missed. No one enquired where he was, as he lay in his bath and smoked the first of a new consignment of Three Castles cigarettes which had just arrived from England.

TWO

The Major's forty-seventh birthday arrived. No one celebrated it, indeed no one knew of it. Had they known, no one would have cared, but the War Office knew, and acknowledged the event with nothing that was remotely congratulatory, but instead it drew the Major's attention to the fact that if he cared to retire, he had thirty years' service in and he was entitled to do so. A copy of this letter was sent to the Commanding Officer, Brigadier Ashton, with an additional, highly confidential letter, asking if it would be in the Army's interest to retain the Major's services and to ask him to sign on for say a further five years, or in the Commanding Officer's opinion, would it be better to part with the Major as soon as it was deemed polite to do so.

The Major immediately wrote to his brother to ascertain exactly what his position would be financially, if he were to retire. He had used his position in India, where he had been for fifteen years, as a money-making system. He had somehow wormed his way into the social side of Army life to such a degree that it had become a full-time job. When he had done it for twelve months, he saw that it could be very lucrative if he gradually made it known that he could be the supplier of high quality items. Many of the young officers came from moneyed families and were used to soft leather saddles for their polo ponies, and they wanted hand-made riding boots, Purdy guns for their tiger shoots, and Savile Row clothes for leisure times. Major Brassington had channelled all the invoices via his brother who was an accountant, and had made sure that there was always ten percent profit, or handling charge. The system worked well and had been running for years, so now was the ideal time to find exactly how well his affairs had been handled. He wrote to John straight away.

Peshawar

19th August 1936
Dear John

I think I am going to retire from HM Forces early next year. I am not much of a hand with mathematics, so just go over my calculations and see if you agree that I can in fact afford to retire.

1 Cash in the Westminster Bank – £7,200
2 My pension will be five pounds and five shillings each week
3 My lump sum as 'thank you' for 30 years service will be £450
4 I have some money here with me and this will be enough to see me through the change from Army to Civilian life. I know there will be hotel bills, clothes to buy, a car etc – but I have enough to cover all that.

So if I bring down the major sum and my lump sum the total will be – £7,650.00

If you can find me the right investment for this sum it might bring me in say just over £200 per year. Please run your expert eye over what I have written and let me know what you think.

Best wishes and I'll meet up with you soon, you can take me to Simpsons on the Strand – one of your clients, I believe.

James

Airmail had just started to and from India and Major Brassington had his reply within two weeks. It was all very reassuring and read as follows:

Clerkenwell

27th August 1936
Dear Jim

Thank you for your letter. Yes your position as regards money looks very good. You will have an income of £10 per week with your capital intact. The average wage here is not more than two pounds ten shillings. A nice house can be bought for £600 in the London area or rented for £1 per week. A nice car costs about £150. I would advise you to look for Salesrooms and Auction Houses for your furniture, no point in buying new. This way they come at one third of the price.

Come and stay with us when you are back in England and yes we will go to Simpsons for lunch, I eat there every Tuesday.

Your luggage will be heavy, so get a car at Tilbury when you dock and bring it all to us. I will help you any way I can.

John

He was home and dry. He wrote back without any reference to Brigadier Ashton, that he would be happy to retire in three months' time. That meant he would arrive back in England in April and have all Spring and Summer to look for somewhere to settle. Brigadier Ashton wrote back to the War Office to the effect that he saw no particular reason why the Army should go out of its way to retain Major Brassington's services. Life on the camp at Peshawar would never be the same again and the Officers' Mess would take a terrible tumble in standards, and Major Brassington would be talked about for years, not because he was missed, but the little luxuries he provided certainly would be.

The Major said nothing to anyone about his decisions. Letters were sent to and from, and confirmation as to his retirement was soon established. He did not tell anyone he was going, but via his servants, he gradually sold many of his possessions: He had two fine horses, some sporting guns, an old car, some furniture, a gramophone, etc. He sold these via his trusted manservant whom he had known for years. He knew him well enough to be certain that he would be lucky to see three quarters of the actual selling price of any of his goods, but the Major was a realist, and that was how things were done in the far East. He had bought them all out of this 'profit', so they hadn't actually cost him anything – this little bout of philosophy suited the situation and he accepted it (and the money) with good grace.

He arrived in England in April 1937, and went to stay with his brother John – the bookkeeper. John lived in Clerkenwell, a busy but none too salubrious area of London. But it suited John because it was easy for him to travel into the centre of London and in particular to the Strand where much of his work was done. The house was big enough to offer the Major a bedroom (he was in fact now a civilian, but it was customary in those days for Field Officers and above to still be referred to by their rank, even though they were actually civilians). The other occupants of the house were a young lady aged about thirty named Lavinia and a boy of seven named Edmond. At the first meal together, around a nice big table in the kitchen, the Major was introduced to Lavinia (who had cooked the meal) and to Edmond. As they all sat round the table together, gradually it dawned upon the Major that John and Lavinia were Edmond's parents; there was no sign of any wedding ring on Lavinia's finger, but they were referred to by Edmond as Mummy and Daddy. It was none of the Major's business at this point, but before too many months had passed it was going to be very much the Major's affair.

Major Brassington spent his time in London reading the more expensive newspapers. He did this in the local library, and he quickly built up a list of addresses of Estate Agents who dealt with country properties. He followed these up, and after twenty or more lengthy conversations he had sufficient information to encourage him to travel to Somerset and to start looking for his own place. He wanted a detached house, with outbuildings, stables possibly, paddocks and grazing land, and the facts he had gathered convinced him that Somerset was where he needed to be.

He called at three offices in Taunton and picked up details of five properties he wanted to look at. He asked where he could buy a car, and was soon in possession of a Morris Ten saloon, and off he went in search of his home in the country. He spent two days looking at the five properties and decided upon one in Curry Rivel, a village about ten miles from Taunton. He told the owner he was interested, then drove to Langport, where he had heard there was a good hotel where he could have a nice meal, a good sleep and take time to reflect upon the Curry Rivel property. The hotel proved to be ideal for all those occupations, and after a hearty breakfast of ham and eggs he drove again to his intended property.

'No, I don't think I will sell it after all,' the owner informed him.

'But surely, it was only yesterday that I was here, and we more or less agreed and fixed a price.'

'Aye – more or less as you says, is one thing, but t'ain't certain, and that's it, and I won't sell to you.'

'Do you mean,' said the Major, 'do you mean you might sell to someone else but not to me?'

'That's my business, not yourn – now I've things to do, so I'll bid you good day.'

The Major went back to his car and thought 'I'll never think well of anybody again.' To follow this way of life would require little effort on his part because his natural inclination was already directed firmly towards such ways of thinking. He drove back to Langport and visited an Estate Agent there, who had just the kind of property Major Brassington was looking for. It was near Somerton, and he offered to take the Major to look at it. The Major would have preferred to go alone, as he hated to be under obligation to anyone, but the Estate Agent gestured towards his car, an Alvis, and the Major loved nice cars.

They discussed the property in detail during the half-hour drive: it was a five bed-roomed house with a big garage, sheds, stabling, paddocks and twenty acres of good pasture land for horses, cattle or sheep, and it was empty and therefore available for immediate tenancy or purchase. The Major couldn't wait to see it, nor was he disappointed when they arrived. The house was good, solid and well maintained. The outbuildings were like most such edifices on English farms – serviceable rather than beautiful – but beauty was not high in the Major's list of priorities. After an hour he said, 'How much is it?'

'To rent it is £8 per week.'

Before the Agent could mention the purchase price, the Major said,

'I'll pay six and guarantee to stay at least two years, and I'll pay twelve months down on the nail.'

'I'll put that to my client, and I'll let you have the answer in two or three days – where are you staying?'

The Major gave him the name of his hotel in Langport.

'Very good – I know the owner – I'll come to see you – soon.'

'The sooner the better. Has it been empty for long?'

'Yes, about nine months.'

'Well then, what are we waiting for? Houses hate being empty, damp creeps in. I want to get in and light some good coal fires.'

'I'll be back to you in a few days,' the agent said as he set the silky smooth Alvis into motion.

THREE

Major Brassington moved into The Olde Farm, Pitney, near Somerton two weeks later. Or, to be more accurate, he started to pay the rent, he was now the official tenant. He spent valuable time in the Auction Rooms of Langport and Taunton and quickly assembled all he needed by way of furniture and carpets. The Auctioneers, who valued his custom and prompt payments, let him have all he needed of blankets, sheets, pillows, tablecloths, cutlery, pots, pans, china etc at decidedly knock down prices, because it was the kind of thing which turned up for them when they had to clear a big country house. All his purchases were now in his home at Olde Farm, stacked in the middle of the large lounge or living room. The Major was not a domesticated person. He knew that the pile of things in his lounge, properly distributed throughout his house, would convert it into a home, but he had not the least idea how to proceed.

The postman called one morning with his post, just as the Major was opening his front door.

'Good morning, Major.' Postmen quickly cotton on to who is who.

'Ah, good morning to you.'

The postman looked beyond the Major and saw the pile of furniture in the lounge. 'I see you've moved in then.'

'Yes I've moved in, and so has all this stuff – I don't seem to make any headway with it.'

'It needs a woman's hand, Sir. They are little marvels at sorting out where to put what. My sister could do that for you, Sir – two or three days and you'd be livin' like a king.'

'Does she live locally?'

'She does, I'll be at her place by lunchtime. Would you like me to ask her Sir?'

'Splendid idea – yes of course – do ask her to come as soon as she can.'

'Right Major – I'll be off now – best of luck.'

The Major went back into the kitchen and decided to disentangle sufficient equipment to make himself a cup of tea.

Two hours later the front door knocker received some pretty harsh treatment, and Grizelda Wainwright stood at the door. Grizelda is a name which is redolent of witches and old hags hovering round cauldrons, and her appearance did little to dispel these thoughts, so the Major got a shock when he answered the door. She announced that she was the postman's sister and she understood there was work to be done.

'Yes indeed, do come in and have a look around and you'll see what the problem is.'

Grizelda viewed the piles of furniture, blankets, sheets, crockery etc and then said 'My brother will have to come and help. Half of this lot needs to go upstairs, and that's man's work.'

'Do go upstairs,' said the Major, 'and then you'll see the bedrooms and you will have an idea of what to put where.'

After ten minutes Grizelda came down and gave her judgement.

'It's Saturday tomorrow so my brother will be off for two days. It'll take all of that to straighten this out – I think you would be better to go to a hotel for the weekend and leave us to it.'

This *was* Major Brassington's house, but before this very powerful lady, and given the domestic nature of all the problems, he was rendered surplus to requirements, and he knew it.

'I think you are right – I would like the bedroom at the back, overlooking the meadows and the lake, but apart from that I will leave the decisions to you.'

'You'd better let me have a front door key, and we'll let ourselves in early Saturday morning.'

The Major meekly handed over the keys to his castle and decided he would go back to the hotel in Langport and seek sanctuary. Formidable ladies such as Grizelda Wainwright brought something new into the Major's life and he felt the best way to deal with it was to go to a comfy hotel and order a stiff whisky.

He returned to Olde Farm on Sunday afternoon about four o'clock. Using his spare key he let himself in. He went straight to the kitchen and immediately noticed two smells very dear to his heart, or dear to his stomach to be more accurate: fresh bread and beef hot-pot. There was no one in the kitchen. He called upstairs and the postman bobbed his head over the rail.

'Hello there Major, come and have a look how we are doing.'

Major Brassington felt a warm feeling creeping over his entire body – he owned a house, nay, a home and he was a proud and happy man.

'This is better than I ever imagined it,' he said loudly as he walked from room to room. His bedroom, overlooking the meadow, now had a fire in the grate. He stood and admired it.

'It will help to drive away any feeling of damp there may be,' the postman said.

'Yes indeed – a kind thought, and the smells in the kitchen – I haven't had a sensation of going into a kitchen and receiving such welcoming smells – no – not since it was baking day when I was a little boy.'

'Zelda is a wonderful cook, can't beat 'er.'

'But there was no food in the house.'

'No, we went out to the shop and bought it all "on tick" for you – we thought you wouldn't mind.'

'I certainly don't mind,' answered the Major. 'It is all wonderfully kind and thoughtful. Is there enough for all of us – you must stay and enjoy it with me.'

At this point Zelda came in. She had been sorting out the outside WC and overheard the invitation.

'Yes please, we would like to stay for a meal. We have worked very hard and are ready for it.'

The Major could not lay any such claims but he was ready for it just the same, and was not disappointed: freshly baked bread and beef stew, followed by many cups of tea. Once the meal was over the Major reached for his wallet. He gave two pounds each to his helpers. They were delighted.

'We have had enough for one day,' said Grizelda. 'I'll come back in the morning and tidy up – if that is all right with you.'

'Yes of course – what time?'

'To do your breakfast if you like.'

'Perfect – about half past seven or eight o'clock.'

Away they went: Grizelda certain that she had a good chance of full-time employment, Edgar the postman pretty sure that he could rely on some additional income as an odd-job man. The Major had noticed that they had placed a comfortable chair in his bedroom, so he poured himself a whisky, picked up his newspapers and luxuriated next to the fire. He was sure he was going to enjoy life at The Olde Farm in Pitney.

FOUR

In London the Gods were conspiring to ensure that the Major's cosy life was to be short-lived.

His brother John's house was three storeys high. The boy Edmond slept on the ground floor. The next floor up was John's office and the main bedroom was on the top floor. A fire broke out in the night and the fumes fatally overpowered John and Lavinia. Most of the rest of the house was saved. Edmond was safely taken out of the house by the fire brigade, and it was left to John's part time clerk to come in and to try to put little Edmond's life together again. In between the fire and the funeral, Fred – the clerk – spent most of his time going over the papers in John's office on the first floor, which was largely undamaged. He realised that Edmond would have to rebuild his life or have it rebuilt for him somehow, so everything which appertained to the little boy he put into a nice new office folder, most importantly his birth certificate, also John's and Lavinia's. There was no marriage certificate.

The Office that Fred was combing through was a mass of filing cabinets and desks. John had run his business as a bookkeeper and accountant for over twenty years, and because he had been involved in tax matters for many of his clients, he had vast amounts of their paperwork as well as his own. Fred had never met John's brother the Major, though he did know of him, and it was not until he stumbled across a small wallet of private papers, a week after the funeral, that he found John's will, which was ten years old, and some very recent correspondence from the Major which advised John that he was now safely moved in and his address was The Olde Farm, Pitney (tel. Pitney 216). Fred drew breath, sat down at the phone, which still miraculously worked, and rang Pitney 216 with the news.

To give the Major credit, the first thing he said upon receipt of the news was, 'And what of the boy?'

'Oh, he's all right, Sir, me and the missus is looking after him, but I have all sorts of papers and money and things. I think you should be here, Sir. I think you are now Edmond's only relative.'

'What about Lavinia's family – could they look after him?'

The Major could see his newly acquired quiet life as the Country Gentleman being given a severe jolt if he had a seven year old under his roof.

'No, Sir. I do remember John saying she was an orphan, and I know that Lavinia, who wasn't all that happy with your brother, if you don't mind me saying so, used to add – but he's all I have in the world.'

'Right – thanks for ringing. I'll see you there early tomorrow morning.'

Dammed irritating – thought the Major. He had spotted a very nice Lea-Francis saloon in a garage in Taunton and he had planned to go and do the deal that day by trading in his Morris Ten.

He took the afternoon train to London, found a hotel not too far from Clerkenwell, and left word at reception that he needed an early breakfast. When he arrived at his brother's house, Fred was there busily sorting more papers. He introduced himself to the Major, and told how he worked regularly as John's assistant one or two days each week and had done for years. The first thing that Fred produced was a parcel containing three hundred and fifty pounds, which he handed to the Major. It *had* contained four hundred and fifty, and Fred kept a hundred pounds, as he explained to his wife, 'nobody ain't paying me nuthin for what I'm doing round there,' and added, 'Who's payin' for 'is keep?' as he pointed to Edmond.

'Quite right too Fred,' agreed his wife, 'you've worked hard for 'im and where's it got you?'

The Major was impressed; three hundred pounds was a lot of money, and it was ready cash which no one knew about. He had expected there to be documents, and he had come prepared with a briefcase, so the cash was put away. Next Fred handed over the will, ten years old but still valid. There was no mention of Lavinia or Edmond (who was only seven years old) and everything was to be left to Captain (as he was then) Brassington. Next Fred handed over the deeds to the house and all the insurance policies, bankbooks and statements. Together the Major and Fred spent the rest of the day combing though great piles of documents. Suddenly the Major said, 'I think you are owed a living out of these papers.'

Fred looked at him in surprise.

'Well for instance, all the papers in that cabinet are concerned with the Savoy Hotel. Now their Accountant and Bookkeeper is dead, they will want all these things to pass on to the next Bookkeeper, and if you can sort all this lot out into the various clients, surely they will express their gratitude.'

'Gratitude is a pretty rare commodity, Sir.'

'Well it is worth thinking about. The phone is there. Why not ring up some of them? Tell them what has happened and that you are working hard to sort things out. Worth trying, don't you think?'

He then slid his hand into the briefcase, withdrew some notes, counted out twenty, thought better of it and added five more.

'Well there's my gratitude anyway. Now let's go to your house, so I can meet your wife and we can talk about what is to happen to Edmond.'

Fred's house was just a walk away and it was obvious from the moment the Major went past the front door that this was a very well tended little home – a big improvement upon how his brother John had lived. Fred's wife came forward to greet the Major with something between a curtsey and a bow. She ushered Edmond towards his uncle and the Major awkwardly put his arm around him.

'I've made something to eat,' Margaret volunteered. 'We'll have it in here, Edmond will be all right in the kitchen. Children's Hour is on the wireless and he likes Toytown.'

The three adults sat around the table where a selection of plump lamb chops occupied the centre, surrounded by bowls of vegetables. Fred's part time occupations: with John, with a Funeral Director and sometimes as a painter and decorator, paid well. They started somewhat uneasily to discuss what to do next, and crucially, who was going to take care of Edmond. Fred was straight and to the point, and the wording of his thoughts left little room for argument.

'You are his family now, Sir, kids are always best with family, and you are his only relative.'

'But he's been brought up around here, won't he miss his friends and his school?'

'No I don't think he will, Sir,' Margaret said. 'He was not really happy at that school, so perhaps at a fresh school, they might know how to handle him.'

'How do you mean, handle him?' the Major asked. 'Is he badly behaved or awkward?'

'No, he is never naughty. Perhaps we would prefer it if he was, but he don't seem to properly get interested in anything. I know John was asked to go to the school by one of his teachers because they couldn't get him involved in anything. He just sits there, as if he's wishin' it was four o'clock.'

'Can he read?' asked the Major.

'Only just, very simple things – I think John said to me one day he was like one year behind all the others.'

'But he is no trouble,' Margaret added reassuringly. 'Very nice manners, quiet you know, but polite, and never in any bother.'

'His is your family, Sir,' Fred said hesitatingly.

'Yes – it does look like it – I'm just trying to sort out in my head how to tackle it. I have someone who comes in to help with the housework, and because I've only moved in recently I haven't got any pattern to my life yet, and what I have organised will have to be re-jigged to accommodate . . .'

He lost the name for a moment. Margaret came to his aid.

'Edmond Sir – 'is name's Edmond.'

'Yes of course – thank you – I admit I am confused – old bachelor you see, and all my career in the Army, I had a batman who looked after my domestic affairs.'

The Major started to laugh. 'Funny isn't it? To be frank I've been selfish and just pleased myself all my life – now I'm going on for fifty and I'm going to have to find room in my life for a backward – would it be fair to use that word? backward child, but he is my own flesh and blood.'

'You never know what's round the corner do you Sir?' Fred said. 'Life is a funny thing, and you never know Sir, you might like bein' a Dad.'

'Well if things don't turn out right, I always said when I was in the Army – I said we'll make the best of it – and that is what I shall do – I know nothing about children – nothing, but I will look after him.'

'He is a nice looking little boy,' Margaret said. 'In 'is Sunday best, he does look a fair treat.'

'Do you mind if he stays with you tonight? It's been a long day, I'll call early tomorrow morning with a cab. If you can get a suitcase packed with all his things – has he any toys or books? – anyway pack them all up, and I'll be here before ten o'clock – tell him what's going to happen – tell him he'll be living in the country.'

'Living in the country' would not mean much to Edmond. His father had pursued his own career remorselessly, unswervingly and with no thoughts about days out, trips to the Zoo or holidays by the seaside. Most Londoners went to Margate or Southend-on-Sea for holidays or days out, but not John, he always had urgent work to complete, and he was tight with his money, so Lavinia and Edmond had been more or less locked into Clerkenwell. It was next to Islington, where there were two or three small parks, but John would have regarded a day out to Regent's Park or Hyde Park as a waste of time and money.

'It is just a trap,' he used to say. 'Just a trap, so as you will spend on ice-cream, pop, sandwiches, and it'll cost you sixpence to hire a deck chair for an hour or two, then it'll rain. No I'm not goin' anywhere.' And they didn't.

Edmond had hardly seen anywhere at all except Clerkenwell, and at that period (1937) it was a busy area, most people were in work. The clock and scientific instrument world was concentrated in that area, so there was work for everybody, but it was poorly paid and most people lived in small terraced houses, with outside WCs. You walked off the street into the living room at most of the houses, which backed onto dingy alley ways at the rear and ill-kept dusty pavements and streets to the front. There was a pub or a little shop at every street corner, usually ill lit by a 40-watt bulb with a flycatcher dangling beneath it. It was a dismal area offering little in the way of stimulation at any level. Edmond was to be removed from this area by his uncle, Major Brassington, and taken by cab (he had never been in a taxi before) to a new life. Fred and Margaret stood at the front door to wave Edmond off and Fred called to the Major, 'Good Luck Boss, let us know if we can help.'

As they climbed into the taxi, the driver said, ' Where to, Boss?'

The Major answered, and off they went.

The Major and Edmond sat in the back of the taxi surrounded by cardboard boxes and a very small suitcase. Edmond was quiet for a while watching the traffic. There was much to see – horse-drawn carts, big red buses, some cars, lorries. Suddenly he turned to his uncle and said,

'Should I call you Boss – like Fred did, and the driver?'

'Yes why not – I suppose you have to call me something – Boss will do fine.'

Edmond resumed his examination of the outside world. It was all new to him. Many things were going to open his eyes. He spent the train journey down to Taunton next to a window. He was fascinated by the bridges, canals with boats on, cows, horses, tractors, trees, fields. His eyes were dancing from one phenomenon to another. Sometimes he would look across the compartment to his uncle to see if he was enjoying the same sensations. The Major just nodded and smiled reassuringly. What was occupying the Major's mind primarily was the fact that Edmond's possessions occupied a lot of this first class carriage and, inappropriately, they were mainly cardboard boxes, tied with up with coarse string.

The Major's car was parked at Taunton Railway Station. He had paid a porter half a crown upon leaving it there, with the request that it be looked after. The same porter saw the Major alighting from the train with a little boy, but his heart sank when he saw the parcels. Despite his title and calling he hated parcels and luggage of any kind, and like most porters of the era usually managed to disappear when trains arrived at the platform. But the Major had spotted him.

'Do bring a truck, there's a good chap. We're going to need some help with this lot.'

The porter's demeanour took on the look of a martyr. 'Me back's not so good today Guv'nor, but I'll do what I can.'

He was really more suited temperamentally to looking after cars than he was to lifting parcels. He pushed the truck towards the Major's car in a manner which gave the impression that the work of carrying the twenty-ton stones which made up the pyramids were child's play compared to his tasks. His breathing as he approached the car gave (he thought) indisputable evidence of asthma, bronchitis, catarrhal blockage, and perhaps more than a hint of impending pneumonia, and he hoped that this display of imminent asphyxiation would lead to the Major taking over the truck and the disposal of the parcels. He began seriously to doubt if he could summon up the strength to hold his hand out for a tip.

The Major had seen 'dodgers' in the Army for thirty years. He opened the passenger door for Edmond and saw him safely in. Walking round to the back of the car he lifted the last two cardboard parcels into the boot, and tossed Edmond's little suitcase onto the back seat of the car. By this time the porter was giving the impression that the mortuary was beckoning, but the shilling pressed into his hand had an amazingly therapeutic effect, and he raised his cap. 'God Bless you Sir – thank you,' and away he went in search of another passenger, preferably one who did not require his services, or one who had featherweight parcels and a heart of gold.

And so Edmond began the drive to his new home. He had never been in a private car before and he had never seen so many country lanes and trees. He was impressed, indeed amazed at the Major's house, which stood back about twenty yards from the road. It was a typical Somerset house with a thatched roof, and the size of about four Clerkenwell terraced houses. The front door was of heavy oak – the sombreness of which was relieved with a brass knocker and letterbox. The windows were mullioned and the builder had thought to use a subtly contrasting stone, which gave the front of the house a decidedly distinguished appearance. The gravel for the drive in–drive out semi-circular drive was a golden colour and this also contributed to the overall picture. Edmond possibly thought he had arrived at a palace. Grizelda opened the front door when she heard the car on the gravel and allowed her face to express astonishment at the arrival of a small boy as well as the Major.

'Who's this then?' she demanded, already seeing her workload doubled overnight.

'This is young Edmond,' said the Major. 'He has lost his parents in a fire in London – he is my nephew and this is now his home, so kindly bring in the parcels from the car, and we'll see about some tea.'

Edmond was shown up to his bedroom. It was about sixteen feet square, in it was a chest of drawers, a big cupboard and his bed. It overlooked the back garden and then the views were of fields, trees and a lake – the latter was not part of The Olde Farm, but it greatly added to the beauty of the view. Grizelda had brought up his parcels and his suitcase and they were scattered all over the floor. He emptied the suitcase first, found the folder with the Birth Certificates in and put this away in a drawer. He then, fairly tidily for a boy, laid out his spare clothes on top of the folder, closed the drawer and began to sort out the cardboard boxes. The contents were mainly books, toys and back numbers of *Dandy* and *Beano*. He put the empty boxes in one corner of the room, climbed on the bed, looked at *Dandy* for ten minutes and fell asleep. He felt safe here at The Olde Farm.

FIVE

The next day Major Brassington walked to the local school and had a brief interview with the Head Teacher. Yes it was perfectly in order for Edmond to start school. He told the Major about the school uniform, but said it was merely recommended but not actually essential. But being a military man the idea of a uniform appealed to him, so he made a note of the outfitters in Somerton where everything was obtainable, and shaking hands with the Head Teacher, he said, 'Right, I'll bring him here next Monday nine o'clock sharp.'

He thought, quite rightly, that for a little boy he had coped with enough changes in the last three or four weeks, and he would now spend some time with his nephew, before launching him into another set of completely unfamiliar circumstances.

The Major went home and found Edmond in his bedroom, looking out of the window. He called to him and said, 'Let's go out for a walk, I'll show you round the village, where your school is. We'll go to the duck pond and feed the ducks, would you like that?'

Edmond nodded and off they went. Just before they left the Major told Grizelda they would be back for lunch. She suggested he might call at the local shop for a few things she needed for the kitchen. She handed the Major a shopping basket with a note in it listing the items required. The Major declined.

'No I'd rather not if you don't mind – not in my line that.' And off they went to feed the ducks.

On the following Monday Edmond started school. Grizelda took him, and promised to come for him at twelve o'clock to take him home for lunch. The Major went into Taunton to see a Solicitor about sorting out Probate for all his brother's possessions. He left the Solicitor with the Deeds of John's house, his bank books, insurance documents, the Will etc and the Solicitor said it would take ten or twelve weeks to sort it out. He then went to the garage where he had seen the Lea-Francis car, saw it was still there, and asked if he could borrow it for an hour to try it out. He was impressed and decided not to trade in the Morris Ten, but to keep the Lea-Francis for best, as it were. He was pretty sure that the total left to him by his brother would make this little extravagance perfectly possible. There was plenty of garage space back at his home, so they could both be kept under cover.

Edmond had now been under the Major's roof for just a few days and a lot of adjusting had to be done. The Major had no experience of children of any age; much less, had he any knowledge of what a newly orphaned child might be going through. He did listen at Edmond's bedroom door for tears or crying out because of bad dreams, but nothing of that sort presented itself. The Major was not a demonstrative person; he had always shied away from 'that sort of thing', hence he was a bachelor. But despite the sort of life he had led in the Army for thirty years, he was not insensitive, and possibly a lot of his brusque behaviour in the Forces was due to a slight imbalance in his personality.

Edmond was having to adjust to a completely different way of life. He did not have anyone now to whom he felt especially close: Grizelda was more than a bit forbidding. He felt closer to Major Brassington, whom he now called 'Boss'. That was really a nick-name, but it brought them closer than addressing him as Uncle would have done, and his trust in Boss was complete. He did feel secure at The Olde Farm. At Clerkenwell with his parents he had always been aware of undercurrents: his mother Lavinia knew they could afford a modest improvement in their lifestyle, days out, picnics, trips to the cinema, perhaps a few days away at the seaside, but John, his father, was determined to make more money. This provided financial security, but it did lead to family squabbles. There was no domestic violence, but actual happiness and open displays of affection were so rare as to be almost non-existent. So occasional walks to feed the ducks usually involved holding Boss's hand, especially when crossing roads, and Edmond found that if he gave Boss's hand a little squeeze it was always reassuringly returned, usually with a glance down from the Major's height, he being a very tall man, and a smile too. Edmond knew he had a friend. Someone who made him feel wanted.

Thus a routine was established at The Olde Farm: the Major pleased himself most of the time. Why not? He was retired, and comfortable for money. Edmond was at school Monday to Friday and Grizelda, who now 'lived in', did everything there was to do.

* * *

The school Edmond went to was a village school. The children stayed there until they were fourteen. There were only six classes, although the children stayed there for nine years. This meant all six teachers had to cope with children who were at different stages of learning. Edmond was seven, nearly eight, but he was in a class where some of the children were nearly nine. The teacher was fully occupied with this system, and his brain often had to be in two or three places at once to cater for the different levels. It was difficult to assess Edmond because he produced so little of anything. His teacher discussed Edmond's attitude to school work with his Head Teacher and they decided that, since he had just lost both his parents, and was getting used to living a completely different way of life, they would have to give him time to adjust. They were very patient and since many of the village children were no great scholars anyway, it was not regarded as anything worthy of special note that Edmond, though approaching eight, was no further on with his studies than two or three of the brighter six year olds.

The teachers at Pitney School all knew from years of experience that the likelihood of any University candidates coming through their system was very remote. Any wealthy or middle class families in the area sent their children to private schools in Taunton or to boarding schools elsewhere. But they prided themselves on helping to form good future citizens who would be well mannered, considerate and sufficiently well educated to enable them to get the best out of life. Certainly all the children would be able to read and write and add up and subtract, and this was sufficient to enable them to take up an active role on leaving school. Most would start work on the family farm, or became apprenticed to a thatcher or a builder. The girls would look for a job in a cake shop or learn to sew.

After a year or so had gone by the teacher did have another word with the Head Teacher about Edmond's lack of progress. This time it had more to do with motivation.

'You see, I can't get him really interested in anything. He is a year, I would say, behind where he should be, but he is not interested in catching up. He seems bright enough and his powers of conversation show clearly that he is not really retarded. He has a brightness about his face which proves to me there is something there, but how do we light the spark?' Mr Swindells, his teacher asked.

The Head Teacher was a very experienced man who through thirty years of contact with children had learnt that there was always room for optimism.

'That is up to us – if there is potential there, Mr Swindells, we have to find it – how it will happen, I do not know. But if you have seen good indications, then keep looking and when the glimmer of light appears, be sure to augment the faint trace with the right encouragement. I am sure you will not fail to notice the signs.'

At his home Edmond was enjoying a varied life – quite different from his time in Clerkenwell. The Major took him regularly to feed the ducks. They went to cricket matches at Taunton and he got a bicycle for his birthday. He had soon found the walk to school was very easy, so Grizelda was relieved of that job after a few weeks. But now he was there and back in no time on his splendid new Rudge.

Major Brassington's standing in the village had taken a tremendous turn upwards shortly after he and Edmond arrived: he decided that the three hundred pounds handed to him by Fred in the ruins of his brother's office did not really belong to him. He took it to the Pitney sub post office and asked if he could open a savings account in his nephew's name. There were three or four pensioners gossiping in the post office at the time and they pricked up their ears. Miss Twyford, who ran the office, got out the necessary forms and asked how much it was for, expecting the sum to be ten shillings or less.

'Three hundred pounds,' the Major said. 'I have the money here.'

The post office emptied as if the gossipers had been sucked out by some freak weather – here was news to be bruited abroad – they could spend many an afternoon on this subject, thus: I was there – I heard him say – for his nephew – three hundred ponds, we heard him didn't we Gracie? Well, I said to Ted . . . etc etc and so it went on for days. This piece of 'confidential' news spread throughout Pitney and its environs. This was news indeed. Three hundred pounds was enough to buy a house and have money left over to furnish it.

When the Taunton solicitor had finished all his calculations regarding probate, the Major was asked to call in for a little meeting, and the figures were laid before him in such a manner that the unwary might well have gained the impression that the total sum – just over two and a half thousand pounds, was in fact a gift from the solicitor to Major Brassington. The solicitor was careful to ensure that his client could see how complicated the correspondence had been, how many phone calls had been made and to what lengths the solicitor had gone to ensure that every penny was safely delivered to its rightful owner. The hope was that the news regarding his fee would not be too much of a shock – two hundred and eighty pounds! The solicitor asked if the Major would like a drink. He rang a bell on his desk and asked for a tray of tea to be brought in; possibly it passed through his mind, if only for a second, that in future he must remember to add 'tray of tea' to his calculations whilst preparing bills. Also it was *just* possible that he had compunction enough to consider whether or not the Major was in need of some kind of recuperative liquid after the shock of the bill.

The Major took the cheque to his bank, and decided that since he liked The Olde Farm so much he would approach the Estate Agent with a view to buying it outright.

It had occurred to the Major that even though the will left by his brother was incontestable, morally Edmond, as John's undoubted son, was his closest relative. But I am forty years older than Edmond and I shall make out my will in his favour, so it'll all be his eventually, his father's money and mine as well. These were the Major's thoughts. With that he went back to the solicitor's office and made out his will, for which he was charged thirty shillings.

'It is the standard charge,' explained the solicitor, somewhat shamefacedly.

Another year passed by. It was now 1939 and there were rumblings in political circles about the possibility of a war. Major Brassington, who was now fifty, wrote to the contact he had in the War Office. He was assured that he would not be called back for service, but they were having preliminary discussions with various politicians about Civil Defence, Air Raid Wardens and the like, and asking him to keep his eye open for notices in the daily newspapers regarding development in these areas. Possibly he would be required to organise something of that sort in the Taunton and Somerton vicinities. War was declared in September 1939; the Major, Grizelda and Edmond heard it on the Major's MacMichael wireless.

'This will change everything,' the Major said. 'You'll see. Nothing will be same from now on. Wars change everything. We're lucky here, out in the country, but towns and cities will be hit – it's a damned shame. Come on Edmond, we'll go and feed the ducks.'

SIX

In the Spring of 1940 the Head Teacher of Edmond's school, Mr Purnell, called a meeting of his staff and made an important announcement.

'I heard on the news this morning that we are all being asked to "Dig for Victory".'

He looked at his six members of staff to see if this had any effect – he saw none, so he continued.

'We have extensive playing fields around this school and we have just over one hundred pupils, many are from an agricultural background. Why can't we dig up some areas and grow food? We have one hundred potential allotment holders here. True, they won't all be keen, but if a half or even a third are, we really could help the war effort.'

Mr Purnell waited a few seconds for it all to sink in.

'You won't dig up the cricket pitch will you? The season will start shortly.' That was one response.

'Where will we get the tools? We'll need spades, rakes, perhaps wheelbarrows too, and seed, I'll bet the seed isn't cheap.'

Mr Purnell was encouraged. Unlike them, he had had to think about the matter, and so he carried on.

'Every year we are given school funds for sports equipment. Well, this year, if you all agree, I'll spend that money on tools for the garden.'

He saw that most nodded agreement, so that was good enough for him.

Another teacher said, 'Many of the parents are farmers. Could we send out a letter telling them of our plans and asking them to spare us some seed?'

'Capital idea, and we'll sow whatever we receive for this first year and see how it goes. We will all learn as we go along.'

'How long do you think this war will go on?' one teacher asked.

'I have lived through the first one and that was four years, so it could be as long as that,' Mr Swindells said. 'Right – it's decision time – the football field is too wet to play, so why don't we cancel football, and R.E., and use those periods for diggings?'

'The Vicar won't be pleased,' someone observed.

'He never is,' laughed Mr Purnell. 'And coaxing the good earth is like a form of praying – so we'll order up some children's spades and make a start as soon as they arrive.'

Each class was told about the plan and, as is bound to be the case when information is handed out to eighteen people, all different responses came out.

'I hates diggin',' was one of the first ones.

'I have a small spade of my own – I help Daddy with it,' was another.

'We'll have to get some horse muck.' That was more positive.

'Don't plant onions on freshly mucked land – my Dad always says,' was another.

Mr Swindells let his class carry on with their comments unchecked for about ten minutes. Then he called them to order. He had enough feedback to convince him that at least half of his squad would have a good try, and he was happy with that.

Mr Purnell, the Head Teacher, and the caretaker spent an afternoon with lengths of two-by-one timber, whitewash and a two-inch brush, marking out twenty areas of land, each measuring twenty feet long by four feet wide with a path three feet wide on every side of every chosen space. It looked like a potential graveyard for twenty-foot coffins. On one of the first available football periods, fifteen volunteers with spades descended upon the putative vegetable plots and began to dig. The rest of the school carried on with whatever was on the timetable. Edmond wasn't too keen on football and he had found a small spade in one of Boss's many outbuildings and decided that he would like to try Digging for Victory. He had discussed it with the Major, who told him he could rely upon a small supply of pocket money, enough to buy some seeds anyway.

One of the teachers, Mr Pendle, was quite a keen gardener and he showed the volunteers, eleven boys and four girls, how to handle their spades. After an hour there was some progress, a few aching backs and one or two blisters, but the great effort to save Somerset from starvation had begun. Mr Purnell, the caretaker and Mr Pendle came back one evening and did an hour or two or three on the plots that hadn't progressed so well, and ten days after the project began, the plots were ready for planting. Fifteen of the twenty plots were the territory of the original fifteen volunteers, the other five were adopted by members of staff, so all were 'tenanted'.

Mr Purnell's letters to parents resulted in a good supply of seeds. Edmond had bought his own, based upon his favourites, so he had potatoes, peas, carrots and onions. Sprouts and cabbage were not among his chosen vegetables, but he probably had enough to cover his plot. Mr Pendle had taken some care to use this new part of the curriculum as an extension of his arithmetic lessons. He prepared charts to show how potatoes, peas, etc should be planted, giving details of spacings. Mr Swindells who was Edmond's teacher, borrowed the charts and made them into a practical demonstration of how useful mathematics can be to solve everyday problems.

'For instance if you plant pea seeds two inches apart across a four-foot bed, how many peas are required for a full row?' He posed this as a question to the class – to his amazement Edmond said, 'Please Sir, twenty-four'.

'That's right Edmond, how did you arrive at the answer?'

'One pea every two inches will let you plant six peas per foot and the bed is four feet wide.'

'That is quite right, so perhaps it would be a good idea if we went now and planted our peas. Have you all got pea seeds?'

Yes they had, or at any rate they knew they could cadge some, and off they went. It was not, strictly speaking, an agreed time for gardening; it was an arithmetic lesson, but Mr Swindells decided to combine it and it was a lovely late March day.

It is difficult to plant across a four-foot-wide bed without standing on it and thus compressing the soil, they would need boards to lay across the plots, but no one can think of everything in advance, and after half an hour hundreds of peas had been planted. Once the planting was over Mr Swindells showed his happy band of helpers how to use a hoe to loosen up the soil they had compacted, and of course to stand back for a minute to admire their handiwork. Their shoes and boots were not looking too good, but he showed them how to scrape and stamp off the surplus, and laughingly said,

'Your Mums won't mind a bit of soil, once you start to take baskets of vegetables home.'

The children made it part of the daily routine, to go and look if anything was 'up'. Even the day after planting all the plots were carefully scrutinised to see if anything was showing through. The fifteen children kept up the daily visit four or five days and then the numbers began to dwindle. Enthusiasm with nothing to fire it does tend to fall away. By the ninth day only Edmond and two friends were continuing the vigil. On the tenth day one little girl pointed to a small pale green shoot, and hooted with delight. Mr Pendle had also decided to come this particular morning and he confirmed that the first ever Pitney School vegetable seed to germinate was undoubtedly Georgina's, and her feeling of joy and triumph was uncontrolled. She ran back to her classroom. The teacher had just started to call the register when she opened the classroom door and screamed,

'The first seed to show through has arrived and it's MINE.' She jumped up and down on the spot and repeated, 'It's mine, it's mine.'

Her teacher tried to instil some sort of decorum into the situation and asked the highly successful horticulturist to sit down. Georgina made her way to her desk, her face glowing with pride and untrammelled hubris. All eyes followed her, and she did not risk any further outbursts, but continued to mouth 'it's mine, it's mine'.

Gradually order was restored and the class paid attention to the work as per the timetable, but for Edmond school was never quite the same again. He could not understand why Georgina had scored such a resounding success, and his plot had produced nothing. The next morning was different. Admittedly, his rival now had a total of four shoots through, but he had seven and Mr Pendle was there to witness it.

'Seven through, Edmond – that is very good, and so is yours, Georgina.' Mr Pendle added this as an afterthought, and then said, 'So Edmond, seven through, how many to come in a row of twenty four?'

Edmond thought for a few seconds and said, 'Seventeen Sir.'

'Quite right young Brassington, quite right.'

As Mr Pendle walked back into school he saw Mr Purnell, the Head Teacher.

'Just been talking to young Brassington and I think your idea about gardening has switched him on.'

'Well I did say it's up to us to light the spark. If this has done it, then I am delighted, he'll be with us for the next five years and we can look for real involvement – that is excellent news.'

The plots were gradually filled up during the following weeks. Some took longer than others because for no apparent reason there are seeds which do not come up. The young gardeners then had to turn their attention to weeding, and some were more attentive than others. The early triumph scored by Georgina may well have given the impression that here was a really keen gardener, but this was not the case, and without encouragement from Mr Pendle and a lot of help from Edmond, her plot would have become weed infested.

SEVEN

Back at The Olde Farm, Major Brassington employed an odd job man two days each week to cut the grass, clean his cars, and sometimes help in the house by tidying out the fire grates and bringing coal into the house. His name was Bert. The Major kept two fine Hunters and it was also Bert's job to attend to the stables. He was retired and liked to keep busy, so he was happy doing odd jobs. He asked Edmond about the gardening scheme at school and received an enthusiastic reply.

'Yes it is great fun, everyone enjoys it,' Edmond told him.

'Well I was thinking,' Bert said, 'of asking the Major if I could do the same here. We have acres of land. The Major doesn't seem to bother about the garden at all, just so long as the grass is cut. I could dig some of it up, and start a vegetable garden here, and of course we have tons of horse manure.'

'Right, Bert,' Edmond said. 'I'll ask Boss tonight at teatime and I'll let you know – do you think I could help you? We could work on it together.'

'That would be very nice, I'd like that. In the summer evenings, after school, we could do an hour or two.'

Boss agreed to this suggestion, and said, 'Right after tea, we'll have a good walk round and find the best place for your new garden, and can we look forward to fresh vegetables this year?'

The Major had not the least idea of how the vegetables arrived on his plate every day – the growing times, the appropriate season etc. He had never given a thought to such things. To be fair, Edmond was hazy as well; he had never really thought about how long it takes for a seed to actually produce a crop. The next few weeks would provide the answers.

Back at the school garden, it was time for pea sticks to be put in place, and Mr Pendle showed the children how twigs about two feet long could be used as supports. The potatoes had to be hoed up and ridged, and there was weeding every day. It was true, there were two or three backsliders, but most of the children came from farming stock, and they knew plants have to be looked after, and what helped everyone was Edmond's enthusiasm. The joy of watching his carrots come through with their delicate leaves like tiny ferns; the more robust potatoes thrusting through and giving promise of that magical new potato flavour. The boy had changed from a nicely behaved but somehow uninteresting child, into one who was becoming the keenest child in the school at every level.

Keenness was not on view all the time. Back at The Olde Farm, Grizelda had overheard the conversations between Boss and Edmond, and they had taken one or two turns that were not quite to her liking. Since the discussions were all about gardening it is perhaps a timely moment to recall that some people like to call a spade a spade, and this is exactly how Grizelda viewed the current situation and possible developments.

She accosted Major Brassington, and as an opener asked, 'Did I hear you aright Sir, when you agreed that some days Bert could stay to his tea?'

'Yes that's right. He and Edmond are going to start a vegetable garden behind the garages, so I thought it would save time if Bert had his tea here.'

'Where, might I ask?' bristled Grizelda.

'Well I hadn't thought of that; with you I suppose.'

It was quite the thing in those days for servants and master to eat separately, but the Major was not one for thinking domestic matters through.

'I might not fancy my tea with Bert – I like my wireless for company.'

'By all means give him his first and you have yours later – he won't mind, but he is going to try to provide for the table, and I would like to help him. The Government has said we must dig for Victory.'

'I don't see how the Government can tell me who I have my tea with.'

'No I don't think they do go in for such minute detail as that, but in wartime we all have to pull together, and this is Bert's idea and Edmond's, and I would like to think that it will be a success.'

'I've known Bert for fifty years, he was just a farmhand, and now he can clean motor cars, and that's about his limit.'

'Well,' said the Major, 'speaking of limits, I've just about reached my limit of discussing what goes on in my own house, and Bert will stay to tea, when he is gardening – is that clear?'

He waited for assent and received a nod. He then went to his study for a pipe of Bruno and a whisky, and under his breath said, 'That bloody woman.'

Major Brassington's property had a lot of outbuildings to it, besides the stables and the garage. Bert had been handyman around The Olde Farm for over a year and on rainy days he had investigated a number of old sheds, partly because he was inquisitive but also, to give him his due, because he did like to be useful. Among his discoveries were about fifty railway sleepers, and Bert saw these now, as the idea of vegetable gardens went around his head, as the edging to the vegetable plots. Built up or raised areas would be ideal. Sleepers are heavy but Bert knew a thing or two about crowbars and how to make a good lever do the work. There was an old four-wheeled trolley in one of the sheds too, and when Edmond arrived home from school, two areas each six foot square were laid out in the chosen vegetable plot.

'This is how we will do it,' Bert began. 'Turn over the sods and chop up the soil, wheelbarrow loads of the well rotted horse manure, and then wheel in more barrows full of soil. I think we should take it from over there,' he pointed to a spot about twenty yards away. 'If we form a basin we can let it fill with water and keep some ducks, and next after that, ask the Major about chickens too.'

'You have been thinking about it,' Edmond said, admiringly. 'You're miles ahead of me.'

'I always wanted a place of my own, but what with the Great War, unemployment in the twenties and thirties and so on, I never did manage it. But now, here, if the Major don't mind, we can play at being farmers every day.' Edmond was nine, Bert about sixty years more than that, but they were like two children, and though nothing was said, they had, tacitly, sworn an oath of friendship.

After the work had been in progress for over a week, Major Brassington came out, with a cup of coffee in his hand, to look how the vegetable plot was progressing. He found the two gardeners hard at it.

'This looks splendid. Where did you find the sleepers?'

'In that shed over there, Sir, there's about another thirty in there.'

'Really? I'd no idea. I thought you had bought them. You must let me know Bert if you are involved in any expense, and I must pay you for what really amounts to overtime.'

'Don't worry about me, Sir – I loves it. Me and my little mate here are having a lovely time. Oh, I was going to ask you about ducks Sir – I've always liked ducks.'

'Ducks – well yes they are lovely, but what about ducks?'

'You see where we are taking soil from over there? After another week or two, when we have filled up some more of these raised beds, we'll have a nice basin there, if I flatten the bottom of the basin with a spade – the soil there is mostly clay you see – it'll gradually fill up and become a pond.'

'You'll have to watch out for foxes – there are a lot around here.'

'Yes I've thought of that. I'll put an island in the middle of the pond. Foxes hates swimmin'.'

'Well then,' said the Major as he strolled away, 'why not chickens as well – I love scrambled eggs.'

Bert and Edmond look at each other with unconcealed delight – it was just as if Christmas had arrived in April. They went on with planting their potatoes with renewed energy. After an hour or so, Bert went to the kitchen and knocked on the window to attract Grizelda's attention. She drew back the lace curtain and non-too invitingly said, 'What do you want?'

'Me and my mate was wondering of there was any chance of a cup of tea?'

'Extra tea is for workers, and anyway I'm busy.'

'You come and look what we've done and you'll agree that we are busy too.' With that Bert walked away.

Purely because she fancied a cup of tea herself Grizelda did make a pot. She took a cup in to the Major, and then two mugs out into the garden.

'Oh this is welcome,' Edmond said. Bert, slurping tea, noisily agreed. Grizelda, cuddling her mug in both hands, cast (as she thought) an expert eye on proceedings and grudgingly had to admit, 'Well it's better than I thought it would be.'

'You won't be saying such like when we are bringing in fresh stuff for you,' Bert said.

Grizelda, determined to have the last word, warned, 'Make sure you don't bring any dirt into my kitchen.'

Work continued until dusk. Bert went home, sucking his pipe, a happy man. Edmond went upstairs and had a half-hour soak in a hot bath.

'Ducks,' he thought, 'and chickens too – me and Bert will have to make a chicken shed.'

When the vegetable garden was finally arranged at The Olde Farm, Bert and Edmond had eight plots, each one six feet square. Seven of the plots were half filled with horse manure and topped off with soil. The eighth one contained only soil. This was to be the onion bed, and Edmond had recalled that onions do not thrive in recently manured land. Edmond wanted to plant seed straight away, but he was restrained by Bert who advised,

'We'll wait a week, 'cos land settles. It'll probably rain too, and that causes land to settle even more. So it is best to wait a bit and that gives us time to get a hut knocked together for the chickens.'

Bert led Edmond to yet another of the many sheds that were part of Major Brassington's property.

'In here,' Bert began, 'there is a little hut, what has been taken apart and laid aside for some purpose, probably twenty years ago, but I reckon there's enough panels to give us what we want, so I think our chicken hut is not that far away.'

They brought out the various pieces of dismantled shed and laid them out on the grass. It was more or less complete, but lacking waterproof materials for the roof, and a good latch and lock for the door.

'I'll ask Boss for those,' Edmond volunteered. 'I'm sure he won't mind.'

'We'll need some boxes too – they likes to lay their eggs, does chickens, in a box full of straw. Apple boxes will do nicely – I'll ask the greengrocer to save us some, and when they start to lay we'll give him a dozen.'

Bert had it all planned out. One of the sheds contained a row of jam jars all full of nails, more or less one size per jar, so no expenditure there. Two days later the shed was up. The local hardware shop dropped off the roofing felt and the latch and lock, and it was ready for its occupants. They didn't have long to wait because Boss spotted an advert in the local paper offering pullets for sale, as they say in the vernacular 'at point of lay'. The owner of the hardware shop saw what Bert and Edmond were doing and advised that the chickens must be kept in a pen. 'Otherwise,' he said, 'they'll be all over the place and difficult to round up in the evening when you want to fasten them up. I can let you have the posts and the wire netting.'

The Major heard all this and approved.

'You come here with the necessary and help to put it up, then let me have the bill. It sounds like good advice to me.'

* * *

So the grounds at The Olde Farm were gradually being changed: eight plots, six feet square were in place. Bert knew a certain amount, but he was no expert. Edmond had only the experience of working his little plot at school where he had concentrated on potatoes, carrots and onions. They needed to be a bit more adventurous. The hardware man mentioned that he had a selection of seeds at his shop, so Edmond called after school to see what was on offer. He stood before the display of seeds and was amazed: four different kinds of radish, three types of turnip, two of beetroot, five different lettuces, two kinds of spring onions. Edmond was stunned, partly by the variety and partly by the realisation that he actually knew so little about this new interest in his life. But he was an 'old customer', so far as the hardware man was concerned, and he came over to help.

'Just keep it simple, that's my advice. Just have one packet of radish, one of turnips – there's hundreds of seeds in each packet. One of lettuce – who wants a lot of lettuce?' he added smilingly. 'Beetroot, they are very easy to grow, and don't forget a bit of colour. Look at these, perennial candytuft, calendula, and poached egg plants. With these you just sow the seeds where you want 'em to flower and they will do the rest.'

He saw Edmond reaching for the French marigolds and antirrhinums.

'Don't go for those, son, they are half-hardies and need special attention, let's keep it simple.'

Edmond's head was spinning – there was so much to learn. He paid for the seed packets, tucked them safely into his pocket, and rode off home on his bicycle.

Normally, when Edmond arrived home from school his first port of call was the kitchen. Usually there was something tasty, even if it was only a crust of freshly baked loaf with some jam on it. But when he arrived home with his seeds he saw Boss in earnest conversation with Bert, so he went straight towards them to see what was going on.

'Ah, there you are Edmond,' the Major called. 'That woman is complaining that the eggs are so small; true enough they are small, Bert was explaining to me that pullets are not fully grown and for a month or two, their eggs are small. But dash it all, she can use three for my scrambled eggs instead of two, there are just so many grumbles.'

'I think the chickens are doing very well,' Bert said. 'We've only got twelve and already we're getting seven or eight eggs every day, how many does she need?'

'What about baby chickens?' Edmond said suddenly.

Bert looked at the Major. 'The birds and the bees' were not a subject which had ever arisen, and it was decidedly not a subject the Major felt happy to pursue. Bert waded straight in.

'We need a cock for that.' Then he stopped and thought for a minute.

'It's like a Daddy hen you see Edmond, same as people, there 'as to be a Mummy and a Daddy hen, d'you see?'

Edmond thought he did, but so much was unfamiliar to him now; seeds, hardy plants, half-hardy plants, cocks and hens.

'I think I'll see if Zelda has got a crust for me,' he said, and went back into the house. Bert and the Major heaved a united sigh of relief and continued discussing the best way to clean the cars.

The chickens now had a pen which was surrounded by a six foot high wire netting fence, so they were safe from foxes, and when they had been established for about a month, Bert arrived with a sack, which seemed to contain troublesome contents. Edmond was just coming out of the hen house with ten eggs as Bert arrived with his burden.

'What's in there Bert?'

'You'll see in a minute – he's a beauty.'

With that Bert entered the pen and released the contents of his sack – a fully fledged arrogant cock-chicken.

'Isn't he a beauty?' Edmond said, as he approached the new arrival to stroke him.

The cock viewed Edmond with that superior eye which few animals or birds can emulate, and he walked away with high steps, as though the ground was tainted. He exuded superiority, and total disdain for his new surroundings. The chickens eyed him warily as they went about their work, scratching up the turf, looking for minute insects. He looked at them as if they were not worthy of his close attention. He then fluttered up on to the roof of the hen house, surveyed his domain, and reluctantly accepted the area, whilst firmly giving the impression that he had expected better. He then let out repeated 'cock a doodle doos' to announce that a new regime was commencing. He was in charge now. He then made a far from dignified descent from the hen house roof, and began to condescendingly peck at some of the corn Edmond was throwing about.

Bert and Edmond smiled at each other. They both knew, but probably could not have put it into words, that exhibitions such as the cock had tried to give, usually resulted in the protagonist looking ridiculous.

'What shall we call him? He must have a name.'

'Well he thinks he looks like a king, so let's call him the Kaiser,' Bert said.

'Good idea,' Edmond said. They had been having some lessons at school about the first Great War, so Edmond knew who the Kaiser was.

'I'll take their eggs in for Zelda, then I'll show you the seeds I've bought.'

They stood next to the eight six foot beds and thought what to do next. Bert began. 'Well that one is full of spuds and so is that, so that's two we got goin'. How about makin' the next one just salad stuff; lettuce and radish?'

That appealed to Edmond's tidy mind, so he laid aside all but the packets containing the salad items and approached the six foot square bed. He was not at all sure what to do next. Bert came to the rescue.

'Let's rake it over so we break up all the lumps and make the soil into a fine tilth.'

'What is that word Bert?'

'Eh, tilth? I believe that's what market gardeners calls it when the soil is fine and ready for seeds.'

'Tilth – I must remember that,' Edmond said. He had just acquired word number one in the vast panoply of words which are essential to any really keen gardener.

'And are we market gardeners then, Bert?'

'Well, no not really, because they grows stuff to take to the market to make a livin', and we are not going to sell ours.'

'No, we are not,' replied Edmond, to whom the idea of selling anything as precious as something one has nurtured was quite unthinkable.

'Right now, once the soil is fine and in grains, we'll lay a board across the bed, so we don't trample the soil flat, and we can start sowin'. Make a straight groove in the soil about nine inches away from the side – keep it straight – that's it. Now open the packet of radish – careful you don't spill 'em. Now pour a few into my 'and.'

'They are like little bullets,' Edmond said. 'Let me feel one. How can it be alive – it is so hard?' He looked at Bert for an answer.

'You are lookin' at the wonder of nature now, young Edmond. There's many things we don't understand. There's lots of clever people at Colleges and they don't know anymore about it than we do. They think they do, and they'll tell you all sorts of things to explain this and that, but nature has 'em all beat. Come and look at this.'

He took Edmond to the farthest part of The Olde Farm land where there was an oak tree of probably three hundred years growth. Beneath it were some of last year's acorns. Bert picked one up. At that point the Major arrived and greeted them with a hearty 'Good Morning'.

'Good Morning to you as well, Sir. I was just explainin' to Edmond that this 'ere tree, which now I would guess weighs two hundred tons, was once – three hundred years ago – just like this,' and he held up the acorn between his thumb and index finger. 'Just like this,' he repeated.

Edmond could think of nothing to say at all. The Major took the acorn from Bert and said 'Amazing! Do you know Bert, I've been on this earth nearly fifty years and I had never given such a thing a moment's consideration.'

'Most people 'avn't, Sir, but I've spent half my life close to the land and it teaches you a lot, Sir – if you don't mind me sayin' so.'

'You're right Bert, you are so right – let's go back to the house, and see if we can coax a cup of tea out of Zelda.'

EIGHT

The garden activities at Pitney School were proceeding, as all gardening does, with mixed results. Some of the children were less keen than at the beginning of the season, but the teachers expected that to be the case, as they would say, 'T'was ever thus'. This philosophy holds good on nature study, cricket, geography, anything. There are always people who start off keenly and then just lose interest. These were the thoughts of Mr Swindells and Mr Purnell as they surveyed the school plots.

'But we have to look at the successes too,' Mr Purnell said. 'The plots aren't lost, we'll just have to re-distribute the available labour, and it might end up with one or two of the children looking after a plot and a half, but that is quite possible.'

'The really keen ones, like Edmond, are probably more enthusiastic than ever,' Mr Swindells observed. 'And though little Georgina's efforts have been inconsistent, she is now one of the best. She and Edmond are real friends, and are always gassing, sometimes in class, about onions and carrots.'

'It's been a good thing. One of the best we have ever done, and I am looking forward to the harvest season. I have spoken to the Vicar, and he is very happy about including the children's efforts in the Church's Harvest Services.'

'Ah! Here come the little gardeners now,' Mr Swindells interrupted. 'Right what is it to be today? I think we should make this a weeding day. Plants always grow better if the weeds are banished. Do you know why this is so?'

Little Michael put up his hand tentatively. 'Is it because it is all tidier?'

'Well, no, that's not the reason why they grow better, but is a good point, just the same. We do want the place to look neat and tidy. No, it's to do with what is in the soil. Plants feed through their roots, just as we feed through our mouths. The goodness which is in the soil makes the plants grow, but if there are weeds in the garden they are taking away the very things needed by the onions and the potatoes.'

'What is the goodness, Sir?' a little voice piped up.

Mr Swindells took a deep breath – you need a deep breath if you are going into deep water and Mr Swindells knew that he was heading there, fast. Mr Purnell heard the question too, but made a tactical retreat to the safety of his Head Teacher's office.

Mr Swindells then delivered himself of a speech which anyone more perspicacious than the average nine-year-old would have known was playing for time: he said 'I will go into the details of that in the classroom, but right now, let's rid our plots of weeds. We'll do the practical now and the theory later. Come on, start weeding. Gently does it, fingers and thumbs are the best weeders ever invented.'

Back in the classroom, Mr Swindells kept strictly to the timetable – he needed time to go to the library in Somerton and look up some reference books. He knew his children well enough to know that they would not let him off the hook. So he went one evening straight after school and spent a very useful two hours soaking up information about plant nutrition, and the various 'do's and don'ts' of plant feeding. Within a week the moment arose: it was a wet morning when they should have been outside gardening and the question came up. The class waited their opportunity and pounced.

'Can you explain the goodness that plants need, Sir?' asked Georgina, a canny little miss, who was hoping that she had Mr Swindells where she wanted him. She was an expert at wearing a look of innocence, as she lured someone into the web she was weaving. 'You see Sir, I can't understand how they know what's good for them and what isn't.'

'Yes, a good question Georgina, you have obviously been thinking about it. But what I want to deal with first is how the goodness feeds the plants via the hair roots, and how they take up water – known as moisture to all gardeners.'

Georgina turned to look at her classmates, she had a subtle smile upon her elfin face – she was really saying, 'he doesn't know – he's waffling.' The look of self-satisfaction on the little madam's face was palpable.

Mr Swindells was unnerved for a minute, but he soon got into his stride and he was off. 'The goodness in the soil is actually tiny particles which have complicated names which scientists use, but we aren't scientists, we are gardeners. If we make sure our plots are watered regularly, either by us, or by the rain, then the particles are released by the soil into the – what is the word we gardeners use? – quite right Edmond – moisture is the word, and so the plant is fed. It may seem strange to us, in fact it is very strange that plants thrive and make food for us out of material we could not possibly eat, such as well-rotted leaves and grass.'

'And horse muck,' came a rustic voice from the back of the class.

'Yes, quite,' said Mr Swindells, now surrounded by sixteen laughing faces. 'Horse manure is vital, but, and it is a big but, only when it is rotted down like the leaves and grass I just mentioned. It is something we all have to remember, that certain things are good for us and some are bad for us – can you think of any examples?'

'Poison is bad for us,' shouted one boy.

'Good food, like bread and eggs. They are good for us.'

'Stew as well – my Mum makes good stew with dumplings in,' came from another contributor.

'I don't like stew,' piped up one little girl, whose Mum was perhaps not quite so expert in that department.

'What about strawberries? Everybody likes them.'

'Some berries are poisonous.'

'Yes that is right, some berries are poison to us and yet birds can eat them.' He knew he shouldn't have said that. He knew he had opened up another can of worms and who should be waiting there but the angelic Georgina.

'We are much bigger than birds, and yet they can eat ivy berries and they would kill us. Why is that, Sir?'

The bell went (saved by the bell), Mr Swindells turned to wipe the board clean, and thought to himself, 'who the hell thought of Dig for Victory anyway?'

Edmond had started a system by which he collected the eggs every morning: he picked up a pudding basin from the kitchen, exchanged a word or two with Zelda, who was never at her best at seven o'clock in the morning, or at any other time for that matter. He then took his dish to the hen house, let out the chickens (and the Kaiser), collected the eggs, usually by now eight or ten of them, and then had a good look at the veg plots. Often he would put down the dish of eggs because a few offending weeds had sprung up over night, and Edmond hated weeds. In the chicken run, the Kaiser usually fluttered up to take up his position on the roof of the chicken hut, where he would announce to the world his undoubted supremacy. No effect at all registered with his harem, they were too busy pecking and scratching. And so the day at The Olde Farm had begun.

Rationing was in force at this time – 1940 – so there was rarely the smell of bacon frying now, but the Major had adapted to this situation and he loved his scrambled eggs on toast. His friend the postman always delivered early to The Olde Farm, so he could open his mail and enjoy a second cup of tea. The Major's mail was usually quite varied: he was involved with the local Hunt, with the Conservative Party, the Home Guard, and with Air Raid Precautions – known as the ARP. They were the volunteers who went round all the houses every night – or more accurately some of the houses every night, to see that the black-out regulations were being observed. As they used to say to any offenders, 'We don't want to show Gerry where we are.' The usual response was 'Who would want to bomb us anyway?' To which the ARP men would say, 'You can't be too careful – they was over Plymouth again last night.' It was all in a good cause and Major Brassington took the work of organising the roster for the ARP very seriously and was quite happy to take his turn, as and when it came around.

Edmond usually joined the Major for breakfast, the conversation was centred upon gardening and in the Major, or Boss as Edmond called him, he found a very willing listener. In fact Boss did more than just listen. He took in what his breakfast companion said, and though he was often slow to show his hand, Edmond's enthusiasm was beginning to rub off on the Major. Edmond left early for school – there was his plot to look at and any invading weeds to be removed. Once Edmond was away, the Major went in search of Bert. His actual work days, that is the days he was paid for were Thursday and Friday, but he came nearly every day: there was weeding to do, chickens to feed and muck out. He was gradually making the putative duck-pond bigger by removing top soil – he was a busy, and happy man.

'Good morning Bert – fine morning.'

'Yes it is Boss.' He had adopted Edmond's mode of addressing the Major, who secretly liked the soubriquet.

'I have been thinking about young Edmond's birthday, and with all this gardening going on, how about a greenhouse?'

'Well I'm sure he'd like one, he'd have a lot to learn if he is goin' to get the best out of it, but he'd love a greenhouse,' Bert replied – privately thinking that he had always wanted one too.

'I'll ask around and see how we can get one made.'

'Old Hardaker is the man to talk to – him who has the hardware shop – he sells timber, glass, putty and such like and his son is a bricklayer – I expect he could build it for you.'

'I'll call in to see him, I have to go that way later today – thanks Bert – have a good day.'

'I will Boss – I'm still making the duck pond area bigger, so I've plenty to do.'

Major Brassington walked to his garage, and had a good look at his two cars, both spotless – thanks to Bert. He decided he would give the Lea-Francis a little run today, and off he went to see Mr Hardaker at the hardware shop. He received full assurance that the materials were available and that Wilf, the bricklayer, had built greenhouses before. Two weeks for it to be up and running was no bother at all, and so it came about that Edmond became one of the very few ten-year-olds to be given a key which would lock the door to his very own greenhouse, and at the same time unlock the door which would lead to a complete way of life.

Edmond opened the door and went into his greenhouse. Wilf had fitted it with benches either side and with extra long window latches – long enough to enable a ten year old to push open the roof lights during hot weather. The Major and Bert waited outside until they were invited in by the owner. Edmond rushed into the Major's arms, shouting, 'Thank you Boss, thank you for a wonderful present – I love it.'

Boss responded by putting his arms around his nephew and gently patting his head. The Major's old Army colleagues would have been amazed at this transformation; from a gruff sarcastic bully to a warm avuncular country gentleman. The old retired Major was enjoying his new way of life.

It was a school day, birthday or not, and Edmond was soon off on his bike, with his key safely tucked away in his pocket. He called at the hardware shop on his way home at mid-day, and asked for a second key to be cut. He then cycled home and presented the duplicate key to Bert.

'Well this is a surprise,' Bert said. 'It's your birthday present you know, not mine.'

'Yes I know, but you are my friend,' Edmond confided to Bert, in the manner known to children, but unfortunately lost to many older people.

'Right, I'll put it with my other keys,' lied Bert. He hadn't actually got any other keys but he wanted to make it sound as appreciative as possible. Bert had lived in the same cottage for years in Pitney, but he had lost track of the keys twenty years before. His views on the subject, if asked, were 'What's the good of locking up, I've nothing worth pinchin' anyway, except perhaps the missus, and who'd want 'er?'

Three days after planting up the salad plot at The Olde Farm, the radish were through. Edmond went along the row examining the little green leaves carefully. 'Three days' he said to himself. 'Three days, and little seeds as hard as pebbles are up.' The lettuce seeds had also amazed Edmond because as he remarked to Bert – 'They look like sawdust, how can they turn into anything?'

'Nature does it – I don't know how, but it is the only answer I can give you.'

'And beetroot seeds too Bert, they just look like little bits of dried up cork. They don't look like seeds at all.'

'No, that's right enough, but they'll be up, you mark my words, and I loves freshly boiled beetroot. Yes, they are all right out of a jar, but I prefers 'em freshly boiled.'

'Like a vegetable.'

'Zackly, like a vegetable. You boils 'em whole roots and stalks, all goes in the pan. If you peel 'em or prepare 'em like you do spuds, they bleeds and goes pale and faded lookin'.'

'Zelda won't like that,' Edmond said. 'She'll say it makes her pans dirty.'

'Ay, she'll find summat to grouse at, you can be sure of that. Now, what is it to be today, this bein' Saturday, we have all day to please ourselves, so what's the main job?'

'I would like to plant something in the greenhouse, but I don't know how to start.'

'Well I've been makin' up little trays out of wood I found in the shed, and I've cadged a few tomato seeds from a friend of mine, so we'll start on that little job.'

'What about the onions?' Edmond asked. 'We will have to grow onions – Zelda says cooking is impossible without them.'

'Well it is a bit late to start them from seed,' Bert said. 'But I don't think we have any choice – we'll plant them seeds today in the greenhouse, they should be up in seven or ten days. Then we'll have to prick 'em out, one at a time.'

Edmond nodded – it was a nod of acceptance, not a nod to indicate that he completely followed what Bert had in mind. The following day Bert turned up at The Olde Farm in a van driven by a friend of his.

Edmond was just returning from his egg collecting duties, when the old van crunched on to the gravel.

'Wait till you see what we got,' Bert shouted, as he opened the van door. They opened the back of the van and there they all were. 'Look at 'em,' Bert cried joyously. 'Tomatoes, onions, runner beans, and French marigolds an' all – we've got a lot of plantin' to do and no mistake.'

Edmond ran into the kitchen, deposited the basin of eggs, and ran out again.

'Come on. Finish your breakfast properly,' Grizelda shouted at him, but he didn't hear a word of it.

'This is very good of you,' Edmond said to Bert's friend.

'I started off too many, allus do, so you're welcome to 'em. I would just have chucked 'em out anyway.'

'Well, as you can see we are making a late start, 'cos I've only just got the greenhouse. I know we are at least a month behind where we should be.'

'Everythin' catches up. You mark my words. Calendars don't know everythin' there is to know about timin' things in a garden. I'll give you a lift, and we'll carry 'em all into your greenhouse.'

There is something of the comrade about gardeners who give plants to their fellow gardeners. It is one of the additional pleasures of being a gardener; it affords the opportunity to share in nature's bounty, to give advice, help, and encouragement and to feel this togetherness in a shared interest. Everyone needs friends in gardening because no one has quite so many enemies: the weather, draughts, too much rain or too little, slugs, vine weevils, wire worms, club root, botrytis – a never ending list.

Edmond and Bert removed a bench from one side of the greenhouse. This was where the tomatoes would be planted. Then they dug a deep trench which they filled with rotted horse manure, covered this with soil and turned on the hosepipe.

'Let's give 'em a really well soaked place to grow in, it give 'em a good start,' Bert suggested. Edmond agreed, though it was all new to him.

'What about the runner beans – are we putting them in the greenhouse too?'

'No. We'll have to put up canes or a frame for them to grow up, but they'll do nicely outside.'

'And these too?' asked Edmond, pointing to the French marigolds, 'where do these go?'

'They are one of my favourite flowers,' Bert confided with commendable patience, 'and I am going to ask Boss, if I – sorry we – can knock up some troughs for around the front door. The front door could do with some flowers around it. They greets you does flowers, when you arrives at somebody's house.'

So with not infrequent tea breaks, the tomatoes were planted (keep the door closed – they don't like draughts, was Bert's advice). They found canes for the runner beans, and after digging trenches for them, they were planted in a sunny spot, each with its own six foot cane, courtesy of yet another of Boss's cornucopia type sheds.

'We'll need to put string between the canes in two or three weeks time, but that will do for today, I'm whacked,' Bert said at about four o'clock. Grizelda emerged from the kitchen, and quite uninvited, went into the greenhouse and examined the tomato plants. She moved to the area where the runner beans were situated, examined the work there, looked at the onion seedlings and presumably approved of the spacing and the straightness of the rows, and then announced.

'There's cheese scones in the kitchen for them 'as wants them, and 'as the good manners to remove their boots.'

NINE

Bert turned up on the Sunday morning, not too early – about half past ten. He saw that Edmond was showing Boss all the additions to the veg plot, and gained a cheery greeting from both. Not so from Zelda who was just coming out with two cups of tea.

'I suppose you wouldn't say no to a cup, if I know you,' she said in her usual manner, but did Bert detect a slight reduction in the abrasiveness of the tone? Was she warming to the idea of fresh vegetables and newly picked tomatoes? No, Bert was quite misled, she was after something.

'You know that friend o' yours who 'as a van? Could he do a job for me?'

'Petrol, you see that's the trouble, it's the petrol,' Bert answered. The Major overheard part of the conversation and asked 'What's all this about petrol?'

'Zelda 'ere wants my mate Gerald to do a job for 'er, but it's the petrol you see, it's rationed.'

'Aye, so is sugar, but you allus says two sugars for me!'

'I can let Gerald have a gallon or two if that will help. What is the journey – how far will he have to go?'

'Aldershot.'

'Aldershot – that's a tidy way.'

'Yes I know it is, but my son's been wounded in the War, and he's due some leave, and what with all his kit, rifle and what not, he'll never make it without a car.'

'OK', Bert said. 'I'll ask 'im – where will he stay?'

'With me', said Zelda, for once without total conviction, because she lived in the Major's house.

Major Brassington assessed the situation, and immediately said 'Of course, sort out one of the spare bedrooms, we must do what we can to help a wounded soldier.'

* * *

Two days later Sergeant Wainwright arrived, with injuries which were by no means obvious and though much emphasised by the sufferer, were, it soon became plain to see, quite spurious. His recall was not good, and a good liar should ensure that he has at his disposal an equally good memory. The injuries moved about with alarming speed and finally settled in his back. A notoriously difficult area for the medical profession to prove or disprove, and a very convenient place for malingerers to hold with both hands and complain of.

The Sergeant rose late and went to bed late. He ate voluminously and washed infrequently. After two weeks, with no correspondence arriving from Aldershot, the Major became suspicious and deliberately timed his breakfast to coincide with his guest's.

'No word from Aldershot then?' the Major asked, 'about your return, possible treatment, long term plans for your recovery?'

'No nuthin'. Haven't had a line from them.'

'They do know where you are – they have this address?'

'Oh yes, I gave 'em this information on the day I left.'

'You do know I was a Major in the Army for thirty years?'

'No. Mother never said that.' The Sergeant began to look worried.

'So I do know about Army Regulations. Have you a sick leave pass, how long it is for, do you have to see a local doctor to have it renewed?'

'Yes they did say something about seeing the local doctor, praps I'll do that today.'

'Yes, I would if I were you, if he gives you a doctor's note, let me have it and if you'll give me the name of your Company Commander I'll send it off for you.'

Sergeant Wainwright grunted some sort of reply and resumed eating the considerable breakfast his loving mother had prepared for him.

In fact the good Sergeant was absent without leave and was awaiting an enquiry into large amounts of meat that had been reported missing from the kitchen he was in charge of. Major Brassington's thirty years in the Army had taught him how to spot a dodger, and he was sure that one such was beneath his own roof. He rang Aldershot and within five minutes was given enough information to confirm his worst suspicions: the Sergeant was in deep trouble and on the run. The conversation was overheard from just outside the door of the Major's study. Wainwright went to the kitchen where the car keys were kept, he helped himself to his mother's purse, which he knew contained the week's housekeeping money for The Olde Farm. He moved quickly towards the Major's garage, tried the keys in the Lea-Francis. They didn't fit, but they did fit the Morris. He started up the car and took it out onto the road. He had little actual experience of driving, and the car was lurching this way and that, but he got used to it and made for Taunton, without any real plan other than escape.

Zelda came into the kitchen and saw the Major. 'I thought I heard you leaving in the car,' she said. 'It just drove out.'

The Major glanced towards the hook where he kept his keys and saw a set was missing. He ran outside and saw the Morris was missing too. He thought of giving chase, but wisely decided that the Police were probably better at that than he was, so he rang the local Police Station.

'Don't worry Sir, he won't get far – we'll catch him.'

'You're right he won't get far, because I don't think there is more than two gallons in the tank.'

'Well then, don't worry Sir, we'll nab him in an hour or two at the most.'

'Watch him, he is a deserter from the Army and he could be dangerous.'

Wainwright soon familiarised himself with the little car, he had driven Army trucks, and after twenty minutes or so, he began to enjoy the freedom of the open road. He drove through Taunton, there was little or no traffic about, and then he decided to make for North Devon. He knew there were hotels at the holiday resorts, and though he had not the intelligence to think up a real plan, he had an idea that arriving at a hotel with a car would give him some status. He could hide up there for a few days and re-think what to do next. On top of Porlock Hill the engine came to a halt, the tank was empty and the little petrol pump which fed the carburettor was ticking away, a sure sign that there was no fuel in the tank. He had just passed the crest of this considerable hill, and decided to let the car roll, in neutral, down the slope, hoping there would be a petrol station at the bottom. This was a heavy little car and it quickly built up speed – 30, 40, 50, 60 miles an hour, Porlock Hill is a very steep long hill, and the Sergeant was panicking. He had never experienced this sort of speed, and it was lucky no one was about and no other vehicles were on the road. He tried to wrestle with the gears, he knew if he could locate fourth, he could, by using the clutch, then force it into third and thus mechanically reduce the speed. He wrenched at the hand brake and stamped on the foot brake but to little effect, though the brake linings gave off clouds of smoke they did little to reduce the speed. At last he found fourth gear, the poor little engine was forced into action, with the car driving it, rather than the opposite. He clumsily exerted tremendous force on the gear lever, when coaxing was what was really needed, and the gear stick came away in his hand.

So in fourth gear, with brake pads now on fire, he careered down Porlock Hill. In front of him, also going down hill, though at a more decorous pace, as befitted his calling, was a Brewer's lorry loaded with barrels. The little Morris hit the back of the lorry, but the collision was cushioned to a certain extent by the fact that the lorry was going at about 20 miles an hour, in the same direction as its 50 miles an hour assailant. The nose of the Morris slid under the rear of the lorry and Wainwright was knocked unconscious. Beer barrels fell off the lorry and began to roll down the hill.

The driver of the lorry stopped his vehicle, jumped out, as well as he could. Most draymen sample their employer's wares as they proceed about their duties, so he was neither nimble nor steady. However his vocabulary was not impaired and he unleashed a sizzling flow of invectives as he went to the rear of his now virtually empty lorry. There he saw the Morris' bonnet, right under the back of his vehicle. Smoke was coming away from the wheels as the brake linings smouldered. Steam from the smashed radiator added to the picture of impending disaster, and there slumped in the front seat was the representative of his Majesty's forces, unconscious. A crash diverted the lorry driver's attention away from the plight of the Sergeant, not that he harboured any tender thoughts about first aid or succour. The crash was caused by four more barrels which had been teetering on the side of the lorry, they fell on to the road and joined their ten or so colleagues in the dash to the bottom of Porlock Hill, two miles away.

A dog noticed the liquid flowing down the gutter and he decided to refresh himself. Judging by the amount he consumed it is safe to assume he was a male of the species. His tail took on a new perkiness, though a second visit to the stream caused his legs to carry him along with little of their usual certainty. Three fellow canines joined him and their tails wagged joyously.

A policeman on his bicycle came upon the scene. He, wisely, was wheeling his official means of transportation because he knew that

Porlock Hill was an enemy of bicycles, it was impossible to pedal up it and damned dangerous to ride down it.

'Well Arthur what have we here?' was his opening challenge to the despairing drayman.

'Silly bugger ran into me from behind. I was goin' along nice and slow, and then BUMP. I hears this crash and blow me if I didn't see beer barrels overtakin' me, and off they went, all the way down.'

'Who's 'ee?' enquired the policeman, no doubt feeling it was up to him to treat this infringement seriously.

'God only knows. I never seen 'im afore and I can't say as how I wants to see 'im again – How am I going to explain this: five 'undred gallons of best bitter down the gutter, and half the dogs in Devon as drunk as Lords.'

'Well I can't arrest dogs for being drunk and disorderly, but you could be in a spot of bother, and as for this Field Marshall 'ere, he's got some explainin' to do, and no mistake.'

The policeman continued his walk down Porlock Hill, no point in hurrying, the main players in the scene halfway down were not likely to go anywhere. He apprised his Sergeant of the situation. Then the police station phone was forced into unaccustomed action: The Sergeant rang for an ambulance, a break-down lorry and he rang the Brewery to tell them of their unfortunate loss, and to assure them that he was doing all in his power to rescue the situation. Sometimes being helpful to a Brewery did pay dividends – the Sergeant was most careful to leave his name . . .

The Major's little car was pronounced beyond repair by the local garage owner, who had his eye on it for his wife. The insurance company paid the Major the estimated value of the car. Sergeant Wainwright made a good recovery and he was soon well enough to take up residence in an Army prison, and Grizelda learned (a little) about contrition and humility.

TEN

The School plots had all reached the time in the season when just the last crop was being picked. Some parsnips and carrots were still growing but little else. The runner beans were still climbing but old, long runner beans are tough and stringy, so it was really time to empty the plots and tidy them up. Edmond wanted to find ways to lengthen the gardening season and he had seen in magazines that it was quite the thing to start off next year's broad beans, and if they over-wintered, which they usually did, then you had a good start on the way to early broad beans. He was prepared to experiment with this, though some of the children were glad gardening was over for the year. Edmond was never likely to become a fair weather gardener, for him gardening was possible, indeed desirable, twelve months of the year.

Back at The Olde Farm, there was no let up at any part of the season: Bert and Edmond had spent a lot of time fully investigating all of Boss's sheds and outbuildings, and had found old cast iron urns and some lead troughs. These were brought out into the open air for the first time in thirty or forty years. After a good rub with a wire brush, they looked very presentable. They decided to leave the lead containers their natural colour, but the cast iron ones they painted white. It was late in the season for any colour in the immediate future, but the ever generous Gerald had surplus wallflowers and so the word biennial moved into Edmond's expanding vocabulary. Gerald explained how the wallflowers needed to be planted in late Spring, given four or five months to mature, and then be planted in September where they were needed to give a show the following Spring. Preferably, Gerald added, interspersed with tulips. Edmond kept a book in his bedroom with these morsels of information carefully written up. Tilth, half hardy annuals, moisture, hair roots, biennials, nutrients. The information was in no particular order, and as the pages filled up, it became a difficult form of reference book. But writing it up, re-reading it, and trying to recall where and how the information was received, all helped Edmond to store the vital facts away – for good.

Subsequent seasons at Pitney School saw Edmond running all twenty plots. His knowledge grew with almost alarming speed, and all the teachers acknowledged and commended the fact that he knew more about gardening after one year than they had learnt in an accumulation of years. He was not intrusive; the other children ran their own plots, but he was always there to help and advise, and the teachers were happy to hand over the responsibility to this single-minded child. The plots became increasingly productive and were widely known in the area. Farmers who had heard of the successes, and possibly had children at the school, would drop off two or three tons of manure. The local hardware man would donate the necessary seeds, and a builder's merchants gave them enough gravel to neatly provide paths between all the plots.

There was no doubt in the teachers' minds as to who was the driving force behind the horticultural success at their school, it was the little boy who went to the plots every morning before school started, and would be seen checking on them after school had finished for the day. He could not spell 'necessary' but he could spell 'chrysanthemum'. He did not have a good grasp of English Geography, but knew that dahlias were from Mexico, rhododendrons from China, and lewisias were from California. What many thought was useless information was the stuff his life was going to be made of.

Mr Purnell was mulling over one of his annual tasks as Headmaster of Pitney: how to find suitable work for his fourteen-year-old school leavers. He had general ideas which he knew would suit the eleven boys and girls who came into this category, but Edmond was a problem. His schoolwork had improved over the last four years. His written work was excellent and beautifully executed. His grasp of arithmetic was very good too, so Mr Purnell had seriously thought about asking Major Brassington if he could investigate the possibility of sending Edmond away to a private school for three or four years to prepare him for University, but an event earlier in the week had set Mr Purnell thinking about what, in the long run, would be best for the boy. The Mayor and various officials had visited the School to make assessments of the 'Dig for Victory' scheme. They knew the part the school had played in feeding many people in the area and so they wanted to acknowledge just how successful the young gardeners were. The local newspapers were involved, so in the life of the school it was quite a big day.

Edmond's success as a gardener was never doubted. The teachers agreed that since the first year, when he was like everyone else, just a learner, Edmond had run the whole project. All the children came to him for advice, which he gave freely, and perhaps more importantly, it was accurate. He was introduced to all the officials and he steered them around the plots. The Mayor was impressed – this boy really knew his subject. He addressed the gathering, as Mayors do, and was full of praise for all their efforts, but he singled out Edmond and asked 'Now you are leaving Pitney School, what do you want to do?

'I am a gardener,' came the prompt reply.

'Ah yes, I can see that, but what do you want to be to earn a living?'

'Just a gardener,' asserted Edmond.

'I see,' said the Mayor. He then walked off with Mr Purnell. 'Is that a problem do you think, the boy wanting to be a gardener?'

'A farmer would be easier, any farmer would take him, but I don't know about full-time work as a gardener.'

'What about the Mortimer place?' the Mayor hazarded. 'They have a massive garden and at least two, maybe even three gardeners from there are in the Army.'

Mr Purnell saw that suggestion as a strong possibility and decided to talk to Major Brassington about it. He met the Major in Pitney the following day and broached the subject.

'I'll give you a cracking reference for him, including a slightly shortened version of what the Mayor said about his efforts,' laughed Mr Purnell.

'Yes, I can imagine it will have to be somewhat edited if that old wind-bag gave a speech – I have met Mortimer a few times at shoots, so he does know me. What's the best way to approach the situation do you think? Could you write to him in the first place?'

The Headmaster agreed to do that, and within a week an appointment was fixed.

The Major was not exactly happy about taking one of his relatives, in all but name, his son in fact, to apply for manual work, but he had witnessed at close quarters just how keen Edmond was on the work, how happy he was doing it, and so he tried the best he could to put aside any thoughts of class and accompanied Edmond to Mr Mortimer's house.

It was called Trehaligan, it had been in the family for over three hundred years and the gardens and land covered about four hundred acres. The gravel drive gave off a lovely crunching sound as the Major's

Lea-Francis found a parking space. The house was four or five times the size of The Olde Farm and it was completely covered with pyracantha and Virginia creeper. It looked welcoming but not particularly well loved – everything was overgrown. Edmond heard a petrol mower doing its duty, and suddenly an old gentleman emerged through the archway in an ill-tended yew hedge, guiding the mower on an erratic but productive path. The mower did not carry any receptacle at the front, so the spray of grass was deposited in front of the mower, and inevitably was picked up again by the blades of the mower as it moved forward.

The Major rang the door pull and Mr and Mrs Mortimer came out to meet him and their future employee. They confessed that the garden had been allowed to go to seed, literally and metaphorically, and that their sole gardener out of four was well over sixty and though very knowledgeable, he was just completely overpowered by the number of tasks which such a large garden inevitably set.

Mr Mortimer then turned to Edmond and said, 'Would you like to try, we would love to have you here, but will it all be too much for you?'

Edmond's answer was surprisingly adult. 'Would you mind if I had a walk around, Sir, so I can see what it is all like?'

'Yes of course – why didn't we think of that? I'll ask Pulkinghorne to show you round. Come outside and meet him, he's been here well over forty years.'

'What did you say his name was, Sir?'

'Pulkinghorne – it's an old Cornish name, they do rejoice in some of the strangest names in this County.'

They went out to find the resident gardener. He emerged again through the archway and responded to Mr Mortimer's gestures.

'This young man might be coming to help you Thomas, so show him around the gardens and bring him back in half an hour or so.'

'Rightio, Sir, I'll look after ee.' And off they went to examine four full years of neglect.

'You keen on gardenin' then?' Pulkinghorne asked, by way of getting the conversation started.

'Yes, Sir, I am, I have worked on Boss's garden – he's my uncle – and I have had a plot at school for four years – but nothing like this.'

'Well no, I don't think there's many gardens in England like this. Before the war, there were four of us full time and we had helpers too at certain times, cherry pickin' and raspberries too, and then there was – well it would go on forever.'

Edmond was a sensitive boy, and he quickly formed the opinion that Pulkinghorne felt guilty at the neglect that surrounded them. This view of the situation was reinforced when the old man's voice took on a sad tone as he recalled the great days before the war. 'We had garden parties 'ere, and over a 'undred people would come. Mrs Mortimer prided 'erself that everything offered was fresh from this garden. All the salad stuff, strawberries, raspberries, nectarines and peaches, grapes an' all. We grew the lot 'ere then.' Pulkinghorne's voice trailed off, as he surveyed the acres of weeds and brambles. Edmond saw him extract a large red handkerchief from his pocket. He made a great fuss of blowing his nose, but there were tears there as well.

Edmond put his hand gently on to the old man's arm and said, 'I would like to help. Do you think we could work together and be friends, like me and Bert do at Boss's place?'

'I've known Bert all my life. Course if you fancy this job we can try together. Don't know as we'll get that much done. An old 'un and a young 'un can't do as much as four fully grown men, but we'll give it a go.'

As they talked, they moved from the immediate area around the house and into the walled garden. It was an area about eighty yards square, all divided up into sections, and with a large circular bed in the middle, full of roses. All were in flower but flopping over each other because they were so sadly in need of pruning or tying up. The other plots – and that was the vast majority of the walled garden – the production area for vegetables and salad stuff, was overgrown and completely unused. They walked further away from the house towards the herbaceous borders, which were in colour but again sadly neglected.

'The orchards is through there,' Pulkinghorne said, pointing to a two or three acre meadow with trees in serried ranks.

'May I have a look please?'

'Yes of course – but it won't cheer you up – they have plenty of fruit on, but prunin' and shapin' the trees was Fred's job and we won't be seein' 'im again, poor beggar – the Germans got 'im.'

Edmond was stunned but not dismayed. He felt very small and insignificant but he still wanted the job – badly.

'Right thank you Mr Pulkinghorne. I'll go back to the house now, and if they'll have me, I'll start.'

'I expect you'll want your four or six weeks summer holidays first,' Pulkinghorne said.

'No – I think I am needed now – I would like to start tomorrow if that is all right with you?'

'Fine with me, you settle it with Mr Mortimer and your uncle first though.'

Edmond went back to the house, found the front door open, went in, heard voices in the parlour and advanced into the room. His face was flushed, his eyes sparkling and his demeanour exuberant. Mr Mortimer rose from his chair.

'Have you seen enough to put you off – I shouldn't be surprised.'

'Oh no, Sir. Quite the opposite. I'd like to start work tomorrow – if I may?'

The Major smiled – he knew his nephew well enough after five years, and he put his arm around him.

'Look after him Mr Mortimer – look after him, he's all I've got.'

With that Edmond and Boss left for home, Bert would be the first to know and Edmond was sure he would approve. No wage had been discussed but Mr and Mrs Mortimer were experienced employers, they had a maid and a cook as well as help in the garden, and they decided nine pence an hour was about right for a fourteen year old. Given a forty-hour week, which was the standard, Edmond would be starting work for thirty shillings a week.

Bert was delighted by the news but at the same time worried that the gardens at The Olde Farm would now be left entirely to him. He mentioned this worry to Edmond.

'No not at all, course not. I love working here with you in our garden. We'll be able to exchange plants. We'll have things they haven't got and vice versa. You'll see it will all work out.'

'What you do expect you'll be doin' as the first job tomorrow?'

'Mr Pulkinghorne, he's the gardener there, told me they have a shed full of tools, wheelbarrows, shears, clippers and so on. I want to get in there and tidy up the shed, and clean up all the tools.'

'Is that Thomas Pulkinghorne?'

'Yes, his name is Thomas.'

'Went to school wi' me, he did, same age as me. He's never worked anywhere else only there. He wasn't Head Gardener you know. No, that was Fred. He got killed in the war. No, Thomas was the general handyman. He could lay flags, knock up a garden seat or an archway, fix a mower, put a new shaft to spade. Did a lot of paintin' too, and roofin'

– you know, shed roofs and such like. Very handy man, but he wasn't really much of a gardener.'

This all left Edmond with mixed feelings. Was he going towards a situation where *he* would have to make all the decisions? This buoyed up his spirits, as he rode on his bicycle for his first day at work. Then as he got nearer to Trehaligan he began to think. What if I can't do it? What if I make mistakes? His conversation had to be diverted at that point, because it began to rain – heavily. He increased his speed, rushing onto Mr Mortimer's gravel, where Thomas waving him into a lean-to shed. He alighted from his bike and brushed the water from his hair and clothes.

'Don't worry son. Somerset rain is not wet, you'll be all right,' said Thomas. 'Come into the next shed – I've got a pot-bellied stove in there. You'll soon be 'avin' your first cup of tea at Trehaligan.'

So the weather decided the priorities of the day: it was so wet that venturing out was impossible, so after his cuppa, Edmond asked Thomas if he could spend the day in the tool shed.

'Good idea too,' came the answer. 'Good clean tools helps every job. Come on we'll make a start.'

The shed did have windows, but the thickness and density of the spider's webs kept out any light. They got the door open and peered in. The tools were beautifully put away, all in their correct places, but they were completely draped in spider's webs, so that the shape of some of the tools was concealed under a gossamer-like covering of webs and dust. It was a diaphanous veil concealing the embarrassed spades, forks and rakes, waiting like spinsters on the shelf. Waiting to be caressed, cared for and given life again.

'If we puts everythin' outside,' Thomas said, 'this rain'll clean 'em up.'

It was still coming down in bucket loads. They laid out all the tools in the rain, and saw the spider's webs and years of dust rinsed off them.

'If we had dusted 'em off inside, we would 'ave been coughin' till Christmas.'

'I'll get a brush and try to clean the windows,' Edmond volunteered.

First he had to move the three wheelbarrows. They objected strongly. They hadn't been moved or oiled for years, and they liked their long periods of inactivity, but he pushed them out in the rain, and then he saw Thomas coming back with a length of hosepipe.

'We'll clean the place out with this,' Thomas cried. 'Then we'll sweep it all out and whitewash it. And look what I've found . . .' It was an old fashioned oilcan with a thumb press. As you applied pressure, oil squirted from its long proboscis. 'Get some old rags, and clean up the tools. A good oilin' will bring 'em up like new.'

Mr Mortimer came out, and saw his two gardeners, both soaked to the skin, sorting out tools, whitewashing the shed, and obviously enjoying themselves. He shook his head, smiled, said aloud 'It takes all sorts,' got in his car and drove off.

By lunch time the shed was whitewashed inside and the windows were clean. It had stopped raining and the two workers surveyed their morning work.

'Not a bad start, I would say,' Thomas said. 'We know what wants doin', and now we know we have the tools for the job.'

At that moment little Betsy came out of the kitchen entrance to the house and said, 'Mrs Bingley says you can come in for your lunch, but you must leave your boots outside – she won't 'ave 'em in, no how.'

Thomas winked at Edmond and said 'What Mrs Bingley sez, goes. Never doubt that young Edmond, else your rations might be cut. Follow Betsy in, and we'll see what today's treat is.'

'Who's this then?' Mrs Bingley asked in a peremptory manner.

'This is Edmond. Mr Mortimer has set 'im on to be a gardener. He'll be with us full time,' Thomas said as he sat himself down.

'Won't be here two weeks,' Mrs Bingley averred encouragingly. 'They comes and they goes.'

Edmond did not answer immediately, but waited until he had sampled the fresh bread and the homely broth, and then made his reply.

'If the food is always as good as this, then I'll be here for long time,' he said, flashing Mrs Bingley a smile between mouthfuls. Mrs Bingley preened herself. Betsy made a face behind her back, and the correct order of seniority in the kitchen was firmly established.

The two happy gardeners returned to their clean tool shed after lunch and started to put the tools away, and then, because visibility was much improved in the shed, Edmond noticed the small chest of drawers in one corner. There were eight layers of drawers to the chest and ten drawers to each layer. Each drawer had at the front a little slot into which a small card could be placed to 'identify' the contents. It was still complete with the cards but they were now all faded. Edmond opening the drawer furthest to the left. A big spider walked out, spun a thread and abseiled to the floor, to go off in search of a new home. Edmond peered into the drawer. It contained a handsome penknife, some pencils, a small pair of scissors with long enquiring tapered blades, a pipe, some matches and a bunch of keys rusted into a solid mass.

'That's Fred's drawer,' Thomas said. ''Ee won't be here no more so you might as well 'ave the penknife – it's a good 'un.'

Edmond took it out of the drawer and felt the weight in his hand. It was large: five or six inches long, it had two blades, and was covered with goat horn either side. It was a quality item. Edmond put it back and opened the second drawer – only another seventy-eight to go. The second drawer contained papers, all folded up. Edmond flattened the sheet out carefully and saw that it was the rotation of crops system for the year 1939. All written out precisely, by someone who was a long way from being a master of calligraphy, nevertheless it was neatly done and eminently readable. Edmond showed it to Thomas.

'Ay, that's Fred's writin', God bless 'im, good chap. He always rotated the crops, he 'ad a system. Onions to follow spuds.'

'How good was Fred?' Edmond asked.

'Well, this is 'ow good he was: he worked as hard as anyone could, and he supervised everything that went on. He was never rattled. I remember once after terrific winds, sweet peas, runner beans, some climbing roses, they was all down flat. He just said see if the stems is cracked off. If they aren't, they'll be all right. So we got 'em up straight – it took us all day, then Fred says right now, an extra generous feed of liquid manure, and leave the hosepipe on all night. A few days later they were all as right as could be.'

'OK,' said Edmond, 'tomorrow morning, if you agree, we'll start on the wall garden, and see how far we get.'

'Perhaps I should have said we had over two hundred foot of runner beans, one hundred of sweet peas and over fifty climbing roses was down – we got 'em all up and runnin'.'

Edmond went through the archway into the walled garden, surveyed the vast area of weeds and brambles and said quietly to himself. 'Well Fred, me and Mr Pulkinghorne will do the best we can.'

ELEVEN

As preparation for the onslaught which was about to begin, Edmond went back to The Olde Farm and spent the evening in his greenhouse, taking out side-shoots from his tomatoes and smelling his fingers. If you can get the real tomato smell from the shoots, the chances are that your tomatoes will have the real flavour.

He was up early next morning, and he pedalled his way to Trehaligan in record time. Tom Pulkinghorne was waiting for him, with a mug of tea at the ready.

'I put an extra sugar in this mornin' – thought we might need it.'

'That's a wonderful start to the day Mr Pulkinghorne, couldn't be better.'

'Let's drop the Mr Pulkinghorne bit – it takes too much breath, and we'll need all the breath we can get, once we gets in there.' Tom pointed to the dreaded walled garden.

'Right then Tom, off we go. Beware all weeds – your end is nigh.'

The sixty odd year old and the fourteen year old went off with a barrow full of tools to begin the rescue of the vegetable garden.

Two of the tools were heavy machetes, dangerous things close at hand, so Tom and Edmund started work on two separate beds, and began to slash through the enmeshed brambles. Hedgehogs lumbered out of Edmund's undergrowth and he took the opportunity to rest for a minute, as they made their way to an adjoining area – hoping for peace and quiet.

Once a large quantity of the brambles and undergrowth had been slashed, Tom suggested they should rake it all on to one bed and set fire to it. This took an hour or so, and then it was ready. Newspapers and a few matches did the rest and they soon had a crackling fire. There was much that was combustible with three or four years of dried up weeds. The two arsonists stood back to admire their fire – all gardeners love a good bonfire. As it subsided they pushed some of the outlying branches into the flames and half an hour later the soil was revealed and it had on it a good layer of potash. The bed surrounds were well delineated with stone and these were in good condition, so Edmond could imagine this bed turned over and looking as it should, but it needed an imagination as vivid as Edmond's to conjure this up.

They started to try to turn over the soil in one of the beds but it wouldn't take a spade.

'Fork is the answer I think,' Tom said.

'You're right. The roots of the brambles are criss-crossed everywhere, but a fork will tease 'em out.'

'And then, onto the embers with 'em – let's keep the fire goin', and burn all the roots we can.'

Betsy came out about ten o'clock with a tray of tea and toast. She was sporting a newly laundered pinny (it was Monday after all) and she looked fresh as a daisy. She laughed as she looked at the two recipients of her hospitality.

'Don't you two look a mess – better not come in at lunchtime, Mrs Bingley would go mad!'

'Ah well, I dare say we do look a bit of a fright, but it can't be helped.'

Tom and Edmond looked at each other and laughed.

'Never mind, it'll wash off and we won't really improve for a week or two – but you'll see – we'll get there.'

Betsy, pert as ever said, 'Yes but where is there?'

After lunch (served out of doors) the two intrepid gardeners began to fork over their two beds, and to throw all the resultant weeds and roots onto another, as yet unstarted, bed. They began to really dig into the two beds and when the roots were removed, up came a crop of potatoes, and it was a good crop.

'Look at this Tom,' Edmond cried. 'Just look how many there are – how can that be?'

'Last sowing in this bed was spuds, and we never took 'em up, so they've multiplied, and with all the weeds on top of 'em, the frost had no effect, so up they comes again.'

'Well, what's Mrs Bingley going to say about this?' Edmond asked.

'Probably,' said Tom, '"I could have told you." No one is allowed the privilege of surprising that one.'

Mr Mortimer was slightly more obliging in his response. He came to the walled garden to look at the progress and said, 'There you are. Half a day's gardening and you have a barrowful of good produce.' He then took out his pocket watch – it was half past two.

'I reckon that is enough for the first day of such a big job. Off you both go now, you've done very well. See you tomorrow morning.'

The next morning began as the previous one had, with Tom awaiting Edmond's arrival with a mug of hot sweet tea in either hand, and a cheery greeting on his lips. They took their drinks through the archway into the walled garden and looked at the two partially rescued beds, and then allowed their eyes to move to the twenty beds not yet started and firmly in the grip of brambles, convolvulus, dandelions, chickweed, and more than a few six foot saplings.

They worked on adjoining beds with their flailing machetes, and soon had the sum total of their chopping and hacking piled on to one bed, newspaper tucked underneath and a merry crackle of another successful bonfire added sparkle to their day. Betsy was a welcome interruption with freshly baked scones and tea at half past ten, and an invitation to soup and Mrs Bingley's special bread at one o'clock.

The two workers stopped at about half past twelve and surveyed the morning work: two more beds were tamed and a good fire was burning. Once that was raked, and then the two beds forked over for the more persistent roots, it would mean that four beds out of twenty had been rescued.

Mr Mortimer came out of the house and looked in to see how things were going. His family had always had money, but Mr Mortimer, not content to live on an unearned income, had run, until he retired, a small business employing thirty people making and repairing agricultural machinery. He was by nature a kindly thoughtful person and therefore a beneficent employer. Some would say 'well he could afford to be couldn't he?' But that does not detract from the fact that he did conduct his affairs in a considerate manner, and he had been a good Manager. He carried these traits into his private life, and to Edmond's and Tom's surprise, he was in the kitchen waiting to enjoy his lunch with them at one o'clock. Mrs Bingley was slightly more officious than usual, if that can be imagined, and Betsy was a little less prone to the giggles, but in other respects the meal proceeded in the usual fashion. When it was over Mr Mortimer asked for a fresh pot of tea, and signalled to the two gardeners to sit down and enjoy an extra cuppa. Betsy foresaw fireworks and made an excuse to go out into the yard. Mrs Bingley made the same assumption and stayed, since other people's discomfort was a source of pleasure to her. She was to be disappointed.

Mr Mortimer began by saying that he could see just how big the job of rescuing the walled garden was going to be, and treading very carefully, he enquired if a suggestion he was going to make would be in order. Both Edmond and Tom nodded. He began. 'This is how I see it. Twenty vegetable plots, in a state of disarray, means a lot of slogging in the next few weeks. So, if I may, I would like to suggest that you do the hard work for half a day, and then plant up what you have rescued for the other half. It is July still – not too late for potatoes, leeks and parsnips, and plenty of time for salad stuff since most of it takes only four to six weeks from sowing to eating – what do you think?'

Edmond and Tom looked at each other and smiled, and then at Mr Mortimer and nodded. They had not thought it through in that way at all. But Mr Mortimer's management skills had not been forgotten. The two gardeners finished their tea, thanked Mr Mortimer for his suggestion, thanked Mrs Bingley for lunch and went back to the walled garden where two beds at least were ready for planting. No ideas came, not right away, then Edmond said, 'This is really rough land, why not treat it that way, and plant as many potatoes as we can. We can plant 'catch crops' of salad stuff in between the rows, and that will fill up the beds and give us the incentive to keep 'em well weeded.'

'Good idea,' said Tom. 'I'll go and ask Mr Mortimer to pick up – what do you think – two hundredweight of seed potatoes? Hardaker never sells out completely, he'll be glad to see the back of 'em, probably let 'em go cheap. I'll look in Fred's chest of drawers, in the tool shed. I know some of the seeds will be two or three years out of date, but sometimes that doesn't matter, they still come up. I know radish and cabbage will, and I think we could try some of the runner beans and peas as well.'

By the end of the day, two beds out of twenty were planted up with vegetable seeds, and the two gardeners, one aged fourteen and one sixty plus surveyed the scene and were pleased with what they had done. Edmond cycled home to The Olde Farm, said 'hello' to Boss and to Zelda, and immediately went out to his greenhouse which was packed with plants, all needing his careful attention. He had three kinds of tomatoes, orchids, scores of coleus, with their multi-coloured leaves, and a Black Hamburg grape vine. Its roots came through the greenhouse wall, so it had access to a plot, just outside the greenhouse, which was twenty feet square and piled with horse manure – this was the driving force for his grape vine and it produced amazing results. It was so fruitful that Edmond had to remove some of the bunches in their entirety and the remaining bunches needed to have about half of the grapes thinned out of each bunch with a pair of special scissors Boss had bought him for his birthday. Then Edmond would look at the raised beds of vegetables, pick out any weeds, have a look at the chickens, exchange aggressive glances with the Kaiser, walk around the duck pond, a trip of about one hundred and fifty yards since the pond was about fifty yards across, and look at the water lilies with their flowers now closed up. This is an aspect of water lilies' normal behaviour, it is as though they consider that they have lavished their beauty on an undeserving public for long enough and they are going to have a rest.

They had never gone to the expense of actually buying ducks, they had just arrived. Firstly a pair of mallards, then some Aylesburys, they lived together happily and all enjoyed the protection afforded by an island in the middle of the pond, which Edmond had planted up with a sequence of flowering shrubs: camellias for March, azaleas for early Spring, amelanchier for a little later and three Japanese acers to ensure that the season ended in a blaze of Autumn colour.

The Major tried at regular intervals to imbue Edmond's life with variety. He was just a little afraid that such single-mindedness was not good for a boy still developing, so he would take him to cricket matches, where Edmond would, after an hour or so, ask 'Boss' if he would mind if he stretched his legs for twenty minutes. Zelda would have packed a picnic basket for this outing and Edmond would make sure that his book of trees was slipped into the container. There are thirty-five trees native to Britain and Edmond wanted to be sure that he knew exactly which they were. Other trees such as sweet chestnut and hazelnut were part of The Olde Farm's stock of trees, so trees from abroad were welcome, but Edmond needed to know which were native to these shores and which were not. After a wander round the cricket field, he would return to sit with 'Boss' and confide in him that he had seen seven different types of tree during his walk. This information was of no use or interest to 'Boss' but he was too polite to give Edmond even an inkling of his lack of enthusiasm. Likewise Edmond upon receipt of details of the scores and who was bowling leg-breaks would respond suitably and with appreciative comments. Civilisation is a wonderful thing and here was a tiny example of it at that most civilised of locations: a village cricket field surrounded by trees.

TWELVE

Two weeks after the rescue of the walled garden had begun, Edmond arrived at Trehaligan house to find Mr Mortimer in earnest conversation with a young man in soldier's uniform.

'Good morning Edmond,' came the greeting. 'Let me introduce you to Philip, he used to work here as a gardener, but as you can see his is now in the Army, and he has two weeks' leave.'

Philip nodded to Edmond, who said, 'Hello.' The next part of the conversation began somewhat stiffly. Mr Mortimer said, 'Philip wants to forget about the Army for two weeks, and he thought, and I agree, two weeks in a garden is about as far away from the Army as one can be.'

Edmond was an intuitive boy, not strictly speaking worldly, but he was sensitive to situations, so he just replied, 'Well there's plenty to do here – I'm sure we can all work together.'

'Who'll decide what we do?' Philip asked.

Somewhere at the back of his mind this was what Edmond had feared. Mr Mortimer did not let him down.

'I'll decide – I'll make sure I'm here at eight o'clock each morning and we'll plan the day together.'

Philip nodded – he did not want a fourteen year old telling him what to do, nor had he much time for Thomas Pulkinghorne whom he regarded as an odd job man. The four went through the archway and into the walled garden where four neatly planted vegetable plots and sixteen unkempt plots greeted them.

'Phew – who let this go?' Philip asked, just a mite aggressively. 'This was always perfect,' and he looked round at poor old Tom accusingly.

'I let it go,' Mr Mortimer said. 'Tom has been here on his own until two weeks ago when young Edmond started, Fred went to the Army like you did three years ago, and as you probably know, we will not have the pleasure of seeing poor Fred again. Wilfred and Bill have been gone for two years, and replacements were out of the question. I did try, but this kind of job does not come into the category known in wartime as essential work. So for two years Tom has done what he could. Just now and then I have had a boy of Edmond's age, but they stayed for no more than a week, and left because they could see no chance of ever getting straight.

'Right,' said Philip. 'Let's get started and we'll see what can be done – leave me to it Mr Mortimer and I'll take over for two weeks.'

Mr Mortimer, for once, did not know what to say. He suspected that Edmond and Tom were in for a rough two weeks, and decided to leave it at that, and keep an eye on the progress, on a regular basis.

There were enough tools in the sheds for everyone, and so Tom and Edmond went for their machetes to begin slashing and hacking in the next beds. Philip watched them for a few minutes. Then Tom stopped for a breather and said to Philip. 'This is how we rescued the four beds.' He gestured towards the four in question. 'We chop everything up, rake it on to one bed, set fire to it and before you knows where you are Betsy is out with tea and toast.'

'Yes I see – I think I'll mow the lawns,' Philip said, and he walked off towards the shed where the mowers were kept. Edmond and Tom looked at each other, shrugged, and fell to with their machetes. Five minutes later the sound of the motor mower was heard, and now three people were working on Trehaligan gardens. Half an hour later the mower came to a halt. Philip came to ask Tom where the petrol was kept and was told that the petrol was strictly rationed and only Mr Mortimer could sanction its use.

'Ok, I'll use the other one.' He pointed to Edmond and said, 'Come and help me.'

The machine he was referring to was a beautifully made old fashioned mower designed so that two people were need to operate it: one behind, pushing and guiding it, and one in front pulling on a rope which was attached to the front of the mower. It required a special kind of relationship to make a success of this method, and it could only be achieved with practice, also a sense of humour helped. This latter ingredient was sorely lacking and Philip soon started to shout at Edmond, who had never done this before and was just not getting the hang of it. Philip was a taller than average, very strong young man. Edmond was a very average fourteen year old, so to work in tandem did require some adjustment, and Philip did not want to concede anything by way of speed.

'Believe me' he shouted, 'when I first started here, if I had pulled like you are doing it, I'd have had my ears rattled.'

Edmond dropped the rope and said quietly to Philip, 'If you don't mind I'll go back into the walled garden now, and we'll ask Mr Mortimer for petrol at lunchtime.'

He left a bewildered Philip to think his own thoughts and he resumed hacking and raking with Tom, who said quietly, 'I 'eard – don't you worry, we'll carry on with this.'

Philip was trying to control his indignation, and seriously wondering whether or not to 'have a go' at Edmond, when Betsy arrived with tea and toast. Her arrival had a miraculously calming effect: she was pretty and the toast was piled high, both qualities certain to bring tranquillity among any trio of males.

Philip opened the conversation in a surprisingly affable manner. 'Do you recall old Mr Harris? He was in charge here for years,' he confided to Edmond. 'Came to work with his trouser bottoms tied up with string.'

'Always wore a bowler hat,' Tom added.

'And a waistcoat, with his watch chain across his stomach. Gold chain he had – leastways he said it was gold. His watch was only silver. He, and only he, decided when it was knockin' off time.'

Tom then said 'If anyone asked a question – there were three or four gardeners then, and extra helpers too sometimes – Mr Harris would put his thumbs into his waistcoat, adjust his pipe – he smoked thick twist all day he did – and then he would give forth his answer to the assembled gardeners.'

'I remember once,' Philip broke in, 'he told us how to prune forsythia, just after flowering, he would say, not later in the year or you'll cut off all the next shoots and they are the ones which will flower next year. "You mark my words", he always added.'

'But he knew his job all right,' Tom said. 'And he seemed to be able to forecast the weather. He would look around, check where the wind was coming from and then give his opinion as to what the weather would do tomorrow.'

'And more often than not he was right,' Philip said.

'Where is he now?' Edmond asked.

Tom replied 'If he is alive, he must be well over eighty, but he did retire to just near by, I wouldn't like him to see this place now, it would kill him.'

'You mentioned prunin',' said Philip, 'I think that's what I'll do until the petrol arrives. I noticed some of the rose arches are blocked up for want of prunin', so I'll do that and then give 'em a good feed and put the hose pipe to 'em.'

'Bring all the clippings here Philip,' Tom said, 'and we'll get rid of 'em on the fire.'

In an hour or so Philip arrived with a barrowload of rose clippings. Edmond decided to sort out thirty or so of the healthier looking stems and then he threw the rest on the fire.

'What's these for?' Tom asked Edmond.

'I'm going to plant them as cuttings – I read somewhere that it takes about twelve months, sometimes longer, but they do take if you dig a trench and back fill it with sand or gravel. Mr Mortimer said we were to battle with the vegetable plots in the morning only. So I'll plant some rose cuttings this afternoon. Won't take long.'

The next barrowload of cuttings Philip brought were from wisteria and he said to Edmond, 'Mr Harris used to say that you have to prune wisteria twice, after it has flowered and again in winter. So just you remember that – I won't be here in winter to do it.'

Edmond's store of information was growing, and it was all carefully written up each night in his indexed book and usually cross referenced: so today's piece of new information would be entered in P for pruning and W for wisteria.

Mr Mortimer had an arrangement with the local garage and he bought his petrol at Black Market price. He didn't like it, but it was a solution to a problem, and it kept his car going and his motor mower. Philip used the mower correctly, with the container on the front, and the lawns improved with one cutting. At lunchtime he asked Tom and Edmond if they would mind – just for once – joining him to edge off the lawns. 'It really finishes 'em off,' Philip said. All three of them spent the afternoon with half moon cutters, tidying the edges of the massive lawns and wheeling away the resultant off-cuts.

'Proper job,' said Tom when they had finished. 'That's what Mr Harris would have said. Proper job. He would then have consulted his timepiece and said – right lads, teatime.' And so it was – even without the benefit of Mr Harris' silver watch, Betsy came out with tea and scones – not much butter in times of rationing but all very welcome just the same. Betsy had brought her own cup of tea out and asked if she could join them.

'Well of course,' said Tom, finding an old chair for her.

'There's too much to do out here, especially when Philip has to go back to the Army. I think I might like this kind of work.' Betsy had them all listening intently. 'I saw in the paper yesterday about Land Girls, so if Mr Mortimer agrees, I could be a Land Girl here, and the money's good too,' she added pertly.

'What would Mrs Bingley say?' Edmond asked.

'If Mr Mortimer says "Yes", then it wouldn't matter what Mrs Bingley says, and anyway my sister Sarah is lookin' for a position – I could bring her for my job.'

'You're a proper little manager you are,' Philip said.

'My Mum always says "the Lord helps them who helps themselves".' With that she stood up, straightened her pinny, collected up the trays and walked back to the kitchen.

Two weeks later – Betsy began work as a gardener and her sister Sarah became Mrs Bingley's assistant. The change was not approved of by Mrs Bingley.

'No good will come of this – that's men's work that is. You should be in here helping me, not out there wheeling barrows of stuff around. What about the cold weather? How will you go on when it's snowing and freezing, with your hands all chapped?'

Betsy just smiled and said 'I'll wear gloves.' This was tantamount to a 'back answer', but unfortunately for Mrs Bingley, Betsy was not under her any longer. Sarah was, and for the first few weeks she knew about it.

After Philip had finished his leave and gone back to the Army, the three gardeners moulded into a team. Betsy was sixteen and a very energetic girl, so she could keep pace with a boy of fourteen and a man of sixty plus. She was happy with her choice of work, and glad of an escape from Mrs Bingley's sharp tongue. Mr Mortimer was happy with his team and in order to solidify the arrangement, he made an appointment for a supplier of clothes to come to the house and fit out his three gardeners with new working clothes. All clothes were on a points system but this supplier was happy to sell the clothes provided the majority of the work done by the recipients was agricultural and not horticultural. He measured Edmond and Tom, eyed Betsy's feminine figure and quickly decided it would be slightly indecorous for him to proceed further with measuring and asked if she would be kind enough to call into his shop, where his wife would do the necessary. Two weeks later complete sets of working clothes were delivered to Trehaligan, two sets for each gardener, and the day after the delivery all three turned up for work in their new outfits. Mrs Bingley was horrified; 'that Betsy' had deliberately chosen trousers to work in and she announced to the world that she had never heard of such a thing. All the Land Girls in the country, and there were thousands of them, wore trousers to work, but this made no difference to Mrs Bingley's thinking, and 'to think,' she would say, 'to think that she comes into MY kitchen and eats my soup lookin' like that.'

Betsy had chosen trousers because they had become more fashionable in the last year or two, and she had the kind of figure which filled trousers, but did not end up looking ridiculous. Quite the contrary. Trousers on a lady do say 'look I am a man – I wear trousers – but look a little more carefully, and you will soon change your mind.' Betsy was not unaware of this, and she did like the look of Edmond, so why should she not try to make herself look attractive? Had Edmond been not quite so relentlessly taken up with plants, he might have noticed. Perhaps Betsy too was reticent, so far as flirting was concerned. So romance was not just slow to flourish, it was positively slumbering.

When another two weeks had gone by, twelve of the vegetable plots in the walled garden were safely planted up and receiving regular care. The season of the year was getting later, it was August, and Edmond was very much aware that the perennial borders were looking unkempt. So it was decided at one of the regular toast and tea intervals that at least for a week or two it would be hacking and burning in the mornings and herbaceous borders in the afternoon. Solidago, eremus and heliopsis needed staking and tying up, the delphiniums had flowered once, but Tom insisted that if cut down and watered and fed, sometimes they would come again. So there was much sorting out, dead-heading and pruning to be done. Dead-heading dahlias is not that easy: the new buds are not unlike the spent flowers and Betsy was shown that the rounded buds are the ones to keep and the buds with a little sharp nose are the ones to snip off.

Philip's two week stay had convinced them that mowing with the grass box in front was the way to go, and the cuttings made a handsome addition to the compost heap every week. Edging the lawn added greatly to the 'finished' look of the garden and all the climbing roses which Philip had pruned and fed were budding up for a second flush of colour, so that the arches were now available as archways to walk through, instead of being thorny obstacles. They ruthlessly weeded out the perennial borders, and where the disturbance was more that the plants could reasonably be expected to stand, then they were fed with a general fertiliser and generously watered.

Mr Mortimer was very pleased with his little team of gardeners and Edmond's wage was raised from thirty shillings to two pounds each week. Thomas Pulkinghorne had been drawing the same wage for ten years, but he too received a pay rise, as did the irrepressible Betsy, and as the season drew to a close in the Autumn, Mr Mortimer was rewarded with substantial crops of potatoes, onions, carrots, leeks and parsnips. The apples and pears were picked and laid out in boxes, and the Trehaligan housekeeping bills were reduced each week right through the winter.

Twelve of the twenty beds were rescued and they all produced good crops, and by November Mr Mortimer was looking for further self-sufficiency; chickens were suggested. Edmond told him of the excellent results at The Olde Farm from a dozen or so chickens and Mr Mortimer gave the go ahead for a proper hen pen to be made, and suggested to Tom that two or three pigs would be a good idea too – they had on their land scores of oak trees, and pigs thrive on acorns. The three gardeners, with Tom steering the way – he was an expert handyman – soon became chicken and pig farmers, adding to their workload, but offering wonderful variety to their daily chores.

By the end of Edmond's second year at Trehaligan, the walled garden was back in full production. Two ladies came in part time all through the growing seasons, and they did the bulk of the weeding, edging, tidying and sweeping, whilst Tom, Edmond and Betsy did the slightly more skilled work. All invaded Mrs Bingley's kitchen every lunchtime, and little Sarah did her best to serve everyone with Mrs Bingley's wholesome food and keep Mrs Bingley happy. The latter task had proved impossible for nearly sixty years, so Sarah's chances of success were negligible. Sometimes it did seem that Mrs Bingley's main aim in life was to have people visit her kitchen, but at the same time keep happiness to a minimum and to have joviality regarded as an unwelcome intruder.

THIRTEEN

May 1945 arrived. The War in Europe was over. By August the Japanese had surrendered and the men in the Army were coming home. Philip had worked for Mr Mortimer for five years prior to the War, and he was looking forward to resuming his work at Trehaligan. Wilfred and Bill had joined up about the same time as Philip and they too were expected home at any time. Fortunately Wilfred had spent most of his time in the Army as a driver/mechanic, and he wanted to work in the transport industry, but Bill wanted to carry on being a gardener. Early in September both he and Philip turned up and asked Mr Mortimer if they could restart. For the past three years, the gardens and the general appearance of Mr Mortimer's many acres had been in the care of a rather unusual committee. It consisted of a sixty year old handyman, a seventeen year old boy, a nineteen year old girl and two part time lady gardeners who were also wives and mothers. Their horticultural training added together came to nil, but, by experience, they had learned a lot, and they had transformed Trehaligan from a wilderness into a productive and beautiful garden, where there was now a small pig farm and six dozen chickens. Mr Mortimer exercised his undoubted skills in the realms of diplomacy and took the two applicants into his study, sat them down with a whisky each and outlined the position as to how the outside staff at Trehaligan operated.

Bill had reached the rank of Sergeant a year or so before he was demobbed. Philip was a Corporal, so they were both used to the idea that authority came from above: if the officer said something to Bill, as a Sergeant, he would convey this to his platoon and it would be done – no questions asked. After five years in the Forces they had become used to an authoritarian system of getting work done. Prior to the War they had worked under Mr Harris, and what he said was done – no questions asked. Things had changed and Mr Mortimer was trying to convince these two young men that, gently but consistently, they must change too.

It was a different world now – still a wonderful place to be, with all sorts of new opportunities, but it would not be like it was in the 1930s. Mr Mortimer knew that Philip and Bill each hoped that they would be Head Gardener, and he was convinced that the days of the likes of Mr Harris were over. Not an easy point to put over, but he had sown a few seeds and he hoped they would be so glad to be back home safely that they would gradually adjust to the new ways.

Mr Mortimer was determined to end the interview on a happy note: he handed Bill and Philip an envelope each, which contained two weeks' wages. 'I think we owe you that, you fought for us, and England is still England, thanks to you. So have a holiday, have a rest, and we'll see you in two weeks' time. By then Autumn will be with us, and there'll be a lot to do, plenty of work for everyone.'

Bill and Philip left by the front door of Mr Mortimer's house. They were very quiet. They walked into the walled garden. The massive five thousand square yards of production area were again under cultivation. They walked along the eighty yards of the herbaceous border and could find glorious colour but no fault, and as they went to the rose garden and then the orchard they noticed that all was in order and the five incumbents were cheerfully going about their work. They began to feel 'left out'. They harboured thoughts: were they really needed? Were they being offered a job out of sympathy? Then they walked right into the orchard. The trees were heavy with fruit, but they both saw that the pruning was way short of perfection. The criss-crossing of branches was keeping the movement of air from the centre of many of the trees. Many had not had the codlin-moth treatment. Philip held one of the apples in his hand to show Bill, who nodded to show he knew what Philip meant. As they walked back towards the house, some of the crazy-paving moved and wobbled beneath their feet, and the last one of the oak rose arches was at an angle instead of erect. The Trehaligan 'committee' of the last three years had worked wonders, but the two returning from War to gardening knew there was work, worthwhile and satisfying work here for them, for life if they wanted it.

The two ex-soldiers had their two weeks of freedom and then reported for work. It was late August and time for fruit picking. Philip and Bill had worked on this part of the garden's life before the War and they knew that it was labour intensive. Mr Mortimer had taken a careful look around the orchard and he too had come to the conclusion that they would need everyone to leave their appointed and possibly preferred occupations, and all join in. There were plenty of well-made apple boxes and they had good four wheeled carts, ladders and people. Initially it was all slow to get started, but the team started to gel together after an hour or two. The fruit began to descend, and the boxes began to fill up. The bruised ones were boxed up separately for the pigs, and the larger pears, Comice and Jargonelles, were carefully laid out on soft paper to protect them from damage.

Mr Mortimer told his team at tea break that he intended to try to sell the fruit from the house to callers. 'Before the War,' he explained, 'I used to ship off the lot to the market, where they were sold to the cider trade and to shops. I have made enquiries but I received only a lukewarm response. So, Betsy, would you mind if I set you up at a stall at the front of the house? I will put adverts in the papers and put up posters in the road inviting people to come and buy.' Betsy smiled and nodded. Her attitude was always to give anything a try.

Mrs Mortimer was not nearly so cooperative. 'What will people think? Selling fruit at nine pence a pound – they'll think we're paupers.'

'We will be paupers if we don't take some positive action,' Mr Mortimer replied. 'Wages have gone up. You still have two maids in the house as well as Mrs Bingley and Sarah.'

'Put up the farm rents – there are seven tenant farms on our land. Their rents haven't gone up for years.'

'No, they haven't, and for the very good reason that I haven't done any maintenance on them since before the War. Four of them are thatched, and they badly need re-thatching.'

'What will that cost?'

'Well things have gone up, but I would hazard a guess at seven or eight thousand for the four.'

'Seven or eight thousand for thatching?'

'Yes, that's it. It requires a lot of men to thatch a good sized farmhouse, and one of them has a thatched store house as well.'

'It's thatching over his stores, let him pay for it.' Mrs Mortimer threw out the challenging remark because she had in forty years of marriage never had to think about money, and now she could see the new Armstrong-Siddeley car she hankered after drifting away.

'Nothing is going to be the same now, Florence. The times of the twenties and thirties are gone, and we will have to face up to it together.'

'What *do* you mean? That *I* will have to sell the apples?'

'No, no, it won't come to that, but we will all have to adjust. We have a Labour Government now, and they will do nothing to help the likes of us.'

The stall was set up, with a spare set of Mrs Bingley's weighing scales, boxes of various apples, pears and plums, all priced up, and with Betsy steering the ship, they were ready to meet the public. But few came and takings were small.

'Early days yet,' said Mr Mortimer encouragingly. 'Give it a week or two, then it'll take off.' – And it did. News spread about the quality and about the fact that Betsy allowed the scales to bump down – thus giving an extra apple or pear to each buyer, and the takings rose, especially on Fridays and Saturdays. Betsy hadn't reckoned on working Saturdays – Saturdays were for shopping and getting ready to go to dances, but with Monday 'off' instead and five bob extra, she was happy.

As Autumn crept into winter the gardening jobs all changed: the two part-time ladies signed off until next Spring. The grass didn't need to be cut quite so often – it was back to every seven or eight days instead of every four or five. That did save some time, but aerating is best done at this time, and it hadn't been done at all for four years – then a top dressing and the moss had to be raked off. The apple trees were sadly out of shape, four years had gone by without proper pruning and the grass had been allowed to grow into the twelve foot circle around each tree. Normally this circle would have been kept free of all grass and weeds to ensure that all the rain that fell in the circle would sink down to the tree's roots. There were scores and scores of fruit trees, all needed the circles to be reinstated and then have a rich mulch of compost. The compost was there, and the manure, they now had twenty pigs and about one hundred chickens. It is true there was a strong country smell to all this activity, but as Tom Pulkinghorne said 'You gets all sorts of smells on a farm, but there ain't one of 'em what doesn't give you a good happitite.'

The long herbaceous borders were a bit of a problem for Edmond: they had given good results and were still flowering generously, but the whole border, eighty yards long and ten feet wide, needed digging up, and all the plants, hundreds of them, needed to be split and replanted because they had, in four or five years of neglect, become too congested.

Edmond started at one end and purposely avoiding the peonies which hate any disturbance, he dug up iris, michaelmas daisies, astrantia, golden-rod, marguerites, and working carefully, he introduced fresh compost, and then replanted the healthiest of the off cuts and discarded the parts of the plant which looked tired or diseased. This left him with more plants than he knew what to do with, and as Mr Mortimer came along he noticed that Edmond looked puzzled.

'Is there a little problem here Edmond – you look as though you don't know what to do next?'

'You're right, Sir, I was wondering about all these little plants. I have re-planted as many as we need but these penstemon, for instance, I have about twenty I have no room for, and I have about thirty pyrethrum surplus as well.'

'How long will they keep – you know, before they die off, if you don't plant them?'

'If they are kept damp, I suppose a week would be all right.'

'I'll ask little Sarah to come and help you this afternoon – I've had an idea and it might work. Are there any tables in the various sheds that are easily moved?'

'Yes – there are four or five folding tables in the big shed.'

'Right,' said Mr Mortimer. 'Ask Philip or Bill to help you, and have say two of them lined up near where you are working, and we'll talk about my idea over lunch.'

Over lunch, which became extended, much to Mrs Bingley's irritation, Mr Mortimer outlined his scheme for all Edmond's surplus plants. The gathering around the table listened with various degrees of incredulity and in Mrs Bingley's case with increasing impatience, especially when after forty minutes had gone by Mr Mortimer signalled by pointing to the teapot that emergency rations were needed.

'Nobody I knows buys plants. We just swop 'em between neighbours,' Thomas said.

'That is how it has always been, I admit that,' Mr Mortimer said. 'But this is a changing world, there are a lot of new houses around Taunton, Somerton, and Langport, they all have gardens, and because they are new houses, they have empty gardens.'

'And it's up to us to fill 'em,' Bill said.

'That's the spirit Bill,' cried Mr Mortimer. 'More tea for that man, Mrs Bingley – more tea all round in fact.'

Once the third or was it the fourth cup of tea was downed, Mr Mortimer shepherded his team to the tables near the perennial borders. He was carrying a lot of newspapers under his arm, *The Times* of course, and a ball of string. His gardeners lined up near the tables and Mr

Mortimer tore up the newspapers into suitable pieces, from which a small parcel could be made. This he tied with string and he moved to the next small parcel, and the on-lookers got the idea. Each little parcel was a plant, it was clean and portable and with luck saleable. When he had completed six parcels he said, 'Now do you see what I am getting at? Little plants can be put on the tables where Betsy sells the fruit and perhaps our customers will be tempted to buy a plant as well.'

Mr Mortimer placed adverts in all the local papers and the people came. Some came to buy plants and bought fruit as well, and some did the opposite. They asked Betsy how to plant the small parcels and got the benefit of her two years of experience, which they took as gospel. Each Saturday got better, and though Betsy was entitled to take Monday off, she usually came in to report how things had gone, and to say which plants needed to be made up into little parcels to cope with the next week's demands.

Regular meetings were held, over tea and toast, to decide what to do next. 'Sweet peas are wonderful for cutting – we can set them off now (it was November) and they will get a flying start for next year.' This was Edmond's suggestion and it led to the next stage in their progress as a sales outlet. One couple bought two little parcels of sweet peas and then said to Betsy, 'How tall do they grow?'

'About six or seven feet,' came the answer. 'You need a frame or canes for them to climb up.'

'Do you know where I can buy canes?' the man asked.

Mr Mortimer was passing and he overheard the question, and realised that Betsy had no solution to this problem.

'Just a minute – I'll ask Edmond if we have any to spare,' he said. Five minutes later Edmond appeared with twenty eight-foot canes and a ball of string. He described how to arrange the canes, nine inches apart and how to use the string to make ladders for the sweet peas to climb up.

'How much is that then?' the customer asked.

'Two and sixpence please,' said Betsy. It was as well she was there; Edmond was not so commercial in his attitude as Betsy. Mr Mortimer had witnessed this transaction and was very pleased.

'This is the way to go,' he said. 'We must buy canes, in various lengths, and string too.'

'If we buy hundreds where will we keep them?' Betsy asked.

'Good question – we need a good sized shed, and now we have established ourselves as a place to come for fruit and plants we must move away from the front door.' Mr Mortimer was very much aware that his wife's ideas about money from 'trade' were rooted in the Victorian idea that an income derived from 'trade' was really a lowering of standards.

During the next week a twenty-foot shed arrived and was assembled well away from the front door, and a sign – specially designed by Mr Mortimer, was nailed to the side of it – it read, 'Garden Shop'. The week after, hundreds of canes arrived, balls of string and six spades, six forks, hoes, rakes, hand trowels and two wheelbarrows. Mr Mortimer equipped Betsy with a price list, and because things were sometimes slow he rigged up a bell, which was like a school bell, and customers were invited to ring it to gain attention. It was an understood thing that whoever was nearest to the shed would break off from weeding or pruning and attend to the customer. During the second week, Betsy ran to where the others were working to announce that trading had commenced. She arrived amongst them breathless with excitement shouting, 'I've sold a spade – I've sold a spade.'

Over tea and toast that day the triumph of selling the spade was recalled and the question of what next arose. Suddenly Edmond said, 'Tulips – this is the time for planting tulips. We always keep ours from season to season, but scores of people will not have any at all.'

Mr Mortimer, who often had his breaks with his gardeners, latched on to this and a week later sacks of tulips arrived. Five different varieties, and information was added to Betsy's ever expanding price list. Upon Mr Mortimer's advice Betsy sold them at so much per dozen, but, said Mr Mortimer, 'always make sure you give 'em thirteen – that way they'll be back.'

By the end of November they had sold all their stock of plants and tulips, and Betsy returned to her garden activities, which were never-ending. The deciduous trees had shed all their leaves and this was eagerly awaited by Edmond – he loved the idea of leaf mould. In fact he loved every aspect of making good compost and the idea of returning to the earth all that had come from it appealed to him. All the chicken and pig manure was added in layers to the compost heaps, and the heaps were turned over by hand once or twice each year, and barrow loads of it transported to the orchards. Each tree now lived in the middle of a twelve foot circle – devoid of weeds and luxuriating in a six inch layer of perfect mulch – Edmond's patent compost.

FOURTEEN

Major Brassington was the kind of person who lived a life which could, somewhat unkindly, be said to be prosaic. Flights of fancy and succumbing to sudden impulses were not for him. His life was to a pattern, it was predictable, many would say boring. His Mondays were always the same, as were his Tuesdays. Just occasionally he would deviate, and this would be commented upon by Edmond or Grizelda. He needed routine precisely because he was not an imaginative or creative person. His routine was wrecked when one Tuesday morning – his day to go to Taunton – there was a loud knock on the front door. Grizelda was out at the shops, so he opened the door himself, and there, large as life, was his brother John. The word perplexed is not of sufficient strength to describe the Major's condition: he stood there in silence, rendered speechless and quivering all over with the shock of it.

'Can I come in?' John asked.

'Yes of course, do – I, we need a drink – brandy I think.'

They went into the Major's study where there were two very comfortable Chesterfield chairs.

'You were reported dead in all the papers – I can hardly believe what I am seeing.'

'Aren't you glad I'm not dead? – I am your brother.'

'Yes – of course – it is not a case of not being glad. I am just trying to adjust – I thought I had buried you, and Lavinia. Edmond lives here now with me.'

'Ah, Well – Edmond is a different story – he's not mine anyway.'

'Not yours – what do you mean?'

'He came with Lavinia when I took her in. She already had him before I knew her. In fact when I agreed to take her in, she hadn't said that she had a child. She arrived with her luggage and he was part of it.'

'I think I need another brandy,' the Major said.

'You sit there, I'll get it. I can see you've had a shock – you're quite pale.'

'So what actually happened on the night of the fire – where were you?'

'I was in London, working late – I often stayed the night if I was working on a hotel's books. I just kipped in an empty room, when I got home it was all over. I enquired of a Fire Brigade man, who said the residents in the house both died in the fire and the little boy was safe and being looked after by a man who worked there part-time. I knew that meant Fred, and I knew that he and his missus were nice people, and that they would do the right thing.'

'You went away and left him – never enquired?'

'That's right – he wasn't mine – I told you that.'

'He wasn't mine either – but he is mine now and I intend to keep him, so if you're here to claim him you're too late – he's adopted officially.'

'No, it's all right. I didn't come here because of Edmond, I came to see you.'

'But why didn't you make it known at the time that you were alive – had you something to run away from?'

'Yes. Debt.'

'Debt? I thought you ran a good business.'

'Yes, I did, but Lavinia didn't. She ran a Mail Order Club and it got so big that it was beyond her to run it properly. The amount of cash made her tipsy with the thrill of it and she bungled the whole affair. The Mail Order firm trusted her because she had worked it up into such a big order. So she ordered furniture, watches, clocks, bicycles and such for fictitious customers and then she popped the lot.'

'Popped – what is popped?' the Major asked.

'Pawned of course.'

'But didn't the pawn shop suspect something was amiss?'

'Course they did, but some pawn shops are really just fences – receivers of stolen goods.'

'But your body was found in the wreckage left by the fire.'

'A body was found, I'll grant you that, but it wasn't mine. It was a young lodger we'd taken in just a week or two before. So when the Fire Brigade man said the two bodies found were completely unrecognisable I decided to go missing. Lavinia had always run this Mail Order Club in my name, so they would have been after me for the lot, and I know she had other debts as well. And the taxman was onto me. One of the restaurants where I looked after the books asked me to prepare two sets; one for his use, so as he would know how well he was doing, and one set for the taxman to show how badly he was doing. He fell out with his lady friend, and she shopped him and me to the authorities. I am or was a properly qualified chartered accountant, and if I say they are the facts, then the taxman believes me, but if I betray that trust I am out, and they got me struck off.'

Major Brassington reached for the brandy bottle. He had never heard such a tale of lies, theft, deceit and mishandling in his life. He filled John's brandy bowl as well as his own and began to think about the money which he had sent to John for years whilst in the Army in India – how much had found its way into his account and how much had been embezzled.

'Where have you been, and what have you been doing for the last six or seven years?'

John thought for a minute, sipped his brandy and then launched into his hard luck story. 'I went to Warrington in Lancashire.'

'Strange choice,' the Major said.

'Well, I heard the Yanks had a big depot up there and they were selling off vehicles of all sorts for scrap, and I decided to go into the scrap business. The great thing was most of the vehicles were Army lorries, no use to the Army now because the war was over. But they were easily converted to peacetime use, and new lorries could not be bought at all. So for a few years I did all right, but bigger people with a lot of ready cash moved in and my share got smaller and smaller.'

'How did you find me after all this time?'

'I made friends at one time by buying vehicles from the Ministry of Defence and I got one of my contacts to trace you.'

The straightforward way the Major had always run his life was a million miles away from his brother's methods and he began to wish that he had actually lost his only relative in that Clerkenwell fire. He heard Grizelda coming through the front door and asked her to bring a tray of coffee and a generous plate of toast to his study. He was sure he was in for a long and difficult morning.

With the coffee and toast in front of him the Major settled back to listen to the next episode in this unlikely story. He anticipated a hard-luck story but he didn't get one. John continued on with his adventures in the world of scrap vehicles, but now he had moved to tanks.

'Tanks!' cried the Major in astonishment.

'Yes tanks – they have an amazing number of moving parts – the turret goes round, the gun goes round, they have a lot of wheels which run on the tracks and this means high quality ball bearings. So apart from the two inches of steel and the diesel engine – many of them nearly new, there was always two or three hundred weight of ball bearings. The 'big boys' took my trade so far as the trucks were concerned but I did the business with the tanks and armoured cars, and I was doing very nicely.'

'Was doing, why was?' asked the Major, sure that the crunch was coming.

'Well I suppose all the scrap dealers were running just a little bit contrary to what was strictly ethical, nothing serious, a little case of bribery now and again, but I thought there was honour among thieves. But no, I was running my business out of a briefcase – in other words ready money only and had been doing that for years. I was not paying stamps, tax or anything, no government department knew I was alive. Then one of my so called fellow scrap dealers got caught and he gave 'em my name to help save himself from harsher penalties.'

'What happened then?'

'The National Insurance people gave me a bill for £3,000 arrears of stamps. Well I employed two fitters to take the vehicles apart, and a driver, and I had never paid for any stamps for any of them, and the taxman, after carefully tracing with the Ministry of Defence just how much tackle I had bought over the years, said they would settle for £20,000.'

'Had you made that much?'

'Yes I had, and I had put most of it into a smallish accounts with little local Building Societies – not your Woolwich or Halifax. But it was pay up or prison, so I paid up and here I am, skint.'

'Can't you continue the scrap business?'

'No, I've lost my contacts now and you need a lot of capital. It's all got a lot bigger now – they are trying to sell ships and aircraft – that's big money.'

'So how do I fit into this picture?' asked the Major – fearing the worst.

'Well, you were the beneficiary when the insurance people coughed up, and now you live comfortably here, in some splendour it looks to me, and I would like my money back.'

'Your money has gone on bringing up Edmond. The cost of living, of running a house, has nearly doubled since before the war. I grant you before the war I was comfortably off for money, but an Army pension received before the war is chicken-feed now. I manage, but I have very little capital. I can let you have say five hundred pounds, but no more, and certainly I cannot finance you nor could I afford to keep you.' He added that final sentence because he realised that this shady person, who was his brother, was definitely not the sort of person he could spend his life with.

'So what you are saying is that I can't live here with you.'

'Yes, I am saying that. You just wouldn't fit in here. This is a country life and you are a city person. With five hundred pounds you can buy a small house or a flat in a town or city and get a job as a book-keeper.'

'While you live here in a big house with servants, and part of what is available to you is because of my money.'

'Your money ran out during the war – I'm not a rich man now, and I certainly cannot afford to finance you.'

'Can I stay here for a few days so I can look around for work?'

'No.' The Major was quite definite about that. He was especially thinking about Edmond – would he remember the person who used to be his father? He continued. 'There are plenty of hotels in Taunton, but I would recommend Bristol or Birmingham as places where you are most likely to find your kind of work.'

After a pause Major Brassington said, 'Have you finished your story?'

The answer came in the affirmative.

'Right, well I'll tell you another story now, so listen to this. I am now a Magistrate in this area. I wasn't at first but for the last three years I have been a JP or Justice of the Peace, just dealing with road offences, petty crime, serious debt and so on. Doing this work brings me in contact with a lot of Policemen.'

John's attitude changed noticeably at the word 'Policemen', and he leaned forward and paid attention.

The Major continued. 'There is a Police Inspector here named Unsworth who I often meet at Court, and over a cup of coffee he commented on my name, Brassington and I said to him, yes it is an unusual name. The Inspector then said he had come across it just once before, when he had been a Police Sergeant in East London. The Fire Brigade had contacted his Police Station over a fire in Clerkenwell; two dead people had been found in this three storey house.'

John was gripping the arms of his chair, and his face was contorted with tension.

The Major carried on with his story. 'The Inspector said he was forcibly reminded of these events by my name – Brassington, because that was the name of the occupants of the house. The Fire Brigade had called the Police in because they had reason to believe that arson was more than a remote possibility.'

John's demeanour was now best described as frantic, and frozen to the spot. His face was red, almost purple with fright, all caused by unsuccessful attempts to conceal his emotions. The Major noticed the signs, and after a few moments of hesitation he continued.

'The Fire Brigade Officer was a very experienced man, who had fought fires all over London during the war, and the Police Sergeant was an observant and inquisitive officer. They both thought there was something not quite right about the case. It was not straightforward, but the intuitive feelings they both had did not amount to a parcel of evidence.'

The Major waited for all this information to sink in. He poured himself and John a cup of coffee, carefully added milk and sugar, stirring the coffee slowly before he added, 'The information which I have now is between us, it will never be passed on. But in the hands of the Fire Brigade and the Police these facts would be vital to their enquiries. And do not forget – so far as the Police are concerned a case is never closed until it is solved. What I think is of no concern to anyone, but what would the Police conclude if a property is burnt out, and the owner goes missing and prefers to have himself presumed dead. They would think this person has something to hide. Especially when he walks away from family, home, money, possessions, and a business. No one does that.'

'Are you saying I did it?' John spat at his brother. He made a grab for the Major's lapels, but he was brushed away as one would a fly. The Major walked to his desk and made out a cheque for five hundred pounds.

'Endorse the cheque pay the bearer,' said John, 'then no one can trace me through the cheque – I'll draw it as cash.'

The Major made the endorsement and showed his brother to the door.

'Goodbye John,' he said.

John folded the cheque and nodded his head. The Major watched him leave The Olde Farm, went into his study and phoned his Bank. He explained to the Manager that this cheque could be cashed – yes he knew it was unusual but he would regard it as a favour. The Bank Manager agreed to do it.

John was never seen nor heard of again. The cheque was never cashed.

Later in the day Edmond came home from his work at Mr Mortimer's house, the Major gave him an unusually warm welcome, but gave no other indication that his day had been anything but perfectly normal. Grizelda made cups of tea and Edmond took his into the greenhouse. The Major stood next to the window cradling his cup in both hands as he watched Edmond who was busy watering little plants in his domain.

FIFTEEN

It was a rainy day and all the gardeners at Trehaligan were soaked. They had all tried their best to ignore the rain, but by midday Tom Pulkinghorne said, 'This is too much, even for us, and by working the land when it is so wet, we are changing our good soil into slush.'

'I'll go to the kitchen', said Betsy, 'and ask Mrs Bingley if we can have our lunch early and in the shed – so we don't all ruin her nice clean floor.'

Twenty minutes later they all felt warmer: Mrs Bingley's beef broth had done the trick and they were warming their hands around big mugs of tea.

Tom said he remembered a day like this over fifty years ago when Mr Harris was Head Gardener. 'Our shed wasn't like this one – in full view – no it was hidden behind yew hedges,' he continued.

'Hidden?' Betsy queried. 'Why hidden?'

'Well that was because Mr Mortimer's grandma ruled this place and the likes of us was not fit to be seen. We were never seen. When we delivered vegetables and fruit for this house, this had to be done before seven o'clock in the morning, and it had to be fresh picked too. So for some of us the day started about half past four in the morning. Course, some of the apprentices – there was always about four of us – would sleep in one of the sheds and wake up two or three times every night to check the temperatures for the melons and pineapples. If there was a snap frost late in May – and we did 'ave 'em sometimes, in fact I recalls one early in June once – why, we had to get up and close the windows to make sure the temperature didn't fall. We got used to it.'

His fellow gardeners received the information in awed silence. Tom continued.

'Her ladyship devised a scheme to make sure we were not seen from the House and it meant that sometimes we had to make a detour of over a mile with the wheelbarrows, right round the back of the place where the pigs and chickens are now, just so we would not spoil the view and cause her Ladyship to see anything as uncouth as a mere gardener.'

Again meaningful glances were exchanged by Tom's audience. This was a history lesson, this was news from a different age, and the pupils were far from bored.

'Mr Harris got so he was overweight, course he didn't dig like us, he was in charge and he told us once how his doctor was worried about him and how he put Mr Harris on a diet. Well one day his doctor popped in to see him at his home and he just landed up there as Mrs Harris was serving up Mr Harris' dinner. Doctor says "I thought I put you on a diet." "You did," says Mr Harris, "and I've had me diet, now I'm 'aving me dinner". Nobody told Mr Harris what to do, even them at the big 'ouse was a bit careful with 'im, 'cos of his knowledge, you see.'

'Tell us about the garden parties Tom – I like hearing about them,' Betsy pleaded. Tom was good at yarning and everyone was keen to pass this very wet day as congenially as possible. The wood-burning stove was drying the gardeners out, and a large kettle was on top of it. It had a friendly lid which rattled when boiling point was reached. Tom rose to the occasion.

'I recall once, about 1910, it would be before the first war anyway, I was about twenty I suppose, most of the visitors turned up in horse drawn carriages. The gardeners had been told by her Ladyship – that is Mr Mortimer's grandma, to help un-harness the horses and take them off to a field that was fenced off. Course there was scores of 'em, but they was 'appy enough, we hadn't done the haymaking so it was a good feed for all the 'orses, and there must have been about fifty of them. We'd all been up since half past four, pickin' fruit, and salad stuff. Mrs Bingley's mother ran the kitchen then with three girls to help her, and they was all busy from first thing too, cookin' salmon, crabs, lobster and makin' cakes and trifles. The previous day we had to put up a big marquee – that's a very big tent. The party was Monday, so it was Sunday we put up the marquee – no mention of extra pay nor nothing like that.'

His colleagues looked at each other, aware of and comforted by the fact that they lived in a more considerate age, if it not quite equality, certainly their employer was not a dictator.

'What about the guests – how were they dressed?' Betsy asked.

'The men wore tweed suits and trilbys.'

Betsy cut him short – 'I don't want to know what the men wore. What about the ladies?'

'They looked a treat,' Tom smilingly went on. 'Most had large hats on decorated with feathers, flowers, fruit. One I do recall had a little bird on it – I think it was supposed to be a robin. They were all gentle colours too – the dresses, pale yellow, pink and white. Just one was in black, she'd lost her husband about twelve months before, but it don't stop her getting tiddly by the afternoon and she was seen behind a yew hedge being kissed by one of the young men.' Whoops of delight went up at this news – even the aristocracy were human after all.

'Rules was strict about mourning in them days,' Tom continued. 'Women went into full mourning for two years – veils and all. And then into grey for another twelve months.

'What about men?' Edmond asked.

'Three months,' Tom said.

'Three months,' Betsy spluttered.

'That's right, three months was accepted as a sufficient period of mourning for men. It was what was convenient really – how could a widower with say three young children manage on 'is own? Truth is he couldn't, well a lot of it was hypocrisy anyway. The young lady who was kissing behind the hedge came from a very hoity-toity family but she soon got married again – she had to – if you see's what I mean, and beggin' your pardon Betsy.'

'Granted I'm sure,' said Betsy among all the laughter.

Edmond met his old school teacher Mr Swindells in Langport one Saturday afternoon and since they had much to discuss, Mr Swindells made his way to a little teashop. He asked Edmond how his gardening was going and Edmond asked how the school gardening plots were being handled now, and so the conversation went on for half an hour. The Mr Swindells asked how the sales at Mr Mortimer's Garden Shop were going.

'I don't know all the mathematics of it,' Edmond replied. 'But I do know it is difficult selling border plants because they are awkward things to wrap up as a parcel; by the day after, the paper is soggy and it comes apart. You see we have to keep the plant, if not actually wet, at least moist, and so quite often Betsy – she's the girl who runs the shop, she has to remake the little soggy parcel.'

'Couldn't you sell them in flowerpots? Mr Swindells asked.

'Yes we could, but even small flowerpots are thrippence each and we would need hundreds.'

'So what you need are small containers about as big as a good sized tea cup.'

'Yes, and we need hundreds – I feel that is holding us back, because some customers just don't fancy a parcel which is falling apart.'

'Tins would be the answer.'

'Tins? What kind of tins?'

'You know, Heinz Beans, tinned soup, Bartlett Pears, Pineapple chunks.'

'You're right,' said Edmond. 'That's the answer – but where do we get hundreds of 'em?'

'From schoolchildren of course, at say a halfpenny each – if we could provide hundreds it would help the school funds – I'll talk to Mr Purnell about it on Monday, and if you ask Mr Mortimer what he thinks about the idea I think we could have solved two problems over this cup of tea: how to carry on your business and how to buy the costumes for our next Christmas Show.'

Mr Mortimer was very receptive of the idea and quickly made contact with Mr Purnell, and within a week tins were coming into school regularly from over one hundred families. They were picked up each week by Mr Mortimer, who soaked them in water for twenty four hours to release the tins from their paper labels, and the peonies, marguerites, day-lilies and penstemon could then be sold in what proved to be an amusing as well as useful container. Betsy had a wonderful eye for business and decided that a plant which filled a pineapple chunks tin (always a bigger one) was worth half as much again as one in a standard size. Takings went up and the next problem was how to cope with the extra demand.

During Mr Mortimer's thirty years as a manufacturer and repairer of agricultural machinery he had got to know most of the farmers within twenty miles of Langport and many of them sold off plants in Spring and Autumn of every year. They sold them at the vegetable market at Taunton for whatever they could get. Sometimes it was a lorry load for five pounds, but as far as they were concerned it was five pounds for nothing: they had not had to actually cultivate the plants – they just grew and spread every year. As one farmer said to Mr Mortimer, 'The lane to my place is two hundred yards long and it is lined with Golden Bells.'

'Is that trollius?' asked Mr Mortimer.

'Could be,' said the farmer. 'I don't know, but I cut and bunch hundred of 'em every Spring and I sell 'em at the market wholesale, and then when I've had a good crop off 'em, I dig up most of 'em – not all of 'em mind – I spread out what's left and they all settle down to provide me with next year's crop.'

'Right, next time you dig 'em up – I'll take the lot off you – in fact if you like I'll take the bunches of flowers as well.'

'Right. You're on,' said the farmer. 'And what's more I'll deliver the lot for you.'

When the thousands of plants arrived at Mr Mortimer's house there was consternation: how do they deal with such an enormous problem, it looked like weeks of work. They looked at each other for a solution. Then Edmond said, 'Let's use them like the farmer used them, as a border on each side of the road. The land out to the chickens and the pigs is like a road, it is about five hundred yards. We could rotovate say two feet each side of the lane and plant them there. It will be easy to cut the flowers for selling and next Spring we could dig up say three quarters of them as plants to sell and leave the rest for the following year.'

Mr Mortimer said, 'Yes that's the answer – I'll rotovate it myself – we'll have them in if you'll all work the weekend, and I'll pay the overtime. If we get it all done, we'll all have Monday off.'

The plan worked well and about two hundred of the trollius were left over from the ribbon-planting scheme and were sold at the Garden Shop. The demand was there but the supply was the next problem. Edmond was walking up and down the long herbaceous borders, there were two of them, eight feet deep and each one hundred yards long. They really needed to be re-energized, results hadn't been too good! The borders had not been fed or properly cultivated for years and it showed. Edmond knew there were really large sheets of tarpaulin in one of Mr Mortimer's sheds and he thought he had a plan which could solve quite a number of their current problems. He talked it over with Bert back at The Olde Farm, who advised him to seek Mr Mortimer's approval and backing and thus avoid any possible squabbles with Philip and other workers at Trehaligan. There wasn't actually a Head Gardener. Philip was the oldest, apart from Tom Pulkinghorne, but Tom didn't really regard himself as a gardener. He was a handyman who could do most of the jobs that the word 'handyman' brings to mind, but his memory was not good enough for him to be a gardener. He was not senile, far from it, but real gardeners all have to have phenomenal memories. You can't go to a reference book when you are weeding: you have to know which is geum and which is the weed which looks very like it, or you pluck out the wrong one. Bill was happy now he was demobbed and he was the kind of person who appreciated just how lucky he was to have returned from the war unhurt. The next few weeks would reveal just who was the Head Gardener at Trehaligan, and who would be the undisputed holder of that title for many years to come.

Edmond broached the subject of overhauling the borders by suggesting that he had an idea and would like to discuss it on Sunday morning.

'Sunday morning? Are you sure Edmond? Shouldn't you be having Sunday off?'

'Every day is "off" as far as I am concerned Mr Mortimer, I just love what I am doing.'

'Well all right then – my wife isn't so good at getting up on Sundays, so you come early, say eight o'clock, and I'll ask Mrs Bingley to do us ham and eggs, and then we can discuss your plan.'

Edmond arrived with his 'plan': they were large sheets of paper rolled up, and he laid them at one side as Mrs Bingley herself arrived in the breakfast room with ham and eggs, toast, coffee and hot milk. She somehow gave the impression that Edmond should not really be there and she should not be serving the likes of him. It was there, but it was so subtle that Edmond and Mr Mortimer's enthusiasm for that which they were about to receive meant Mrs Bingley's take on who should and who shouldn't have breakfast in 'the big house' went unnoticed.

With breakfast over, Mr Mortimer eyed the rolls of paper Edmond had brought, and so he asked Mrs Bingley to side away everything from the table, so it could be used to inspect the plans.

'Everything?' queried Mrs Bingley, to whom routine was all important: usually Mr Mortimer lingered over his coffee and had extra pieces of toast. She looked accusingly at the person who had disrupted the Sunday morning norm, but again it was lost, as Edmond began to unroll his plans and dared to use the condiment set to keep the paper flat. She left the room with an exaggerated flounce, but again to no purpose.

The first plan Edmond unrolled was a beautiful representation of the one-hundred-yard border, all in colour, with an index to show which plant was where. Mr Mortimer looked at his young gardener with unconcealed admiration.

'That is a lovely job Edmond, beautifully done.'

'Thank you, Sir. Now this is what I would like to do. I would like to lay three or four large sheets of tarpaulin on the lawn right next to the border, put all the plants on the tarpaulin and then rotovate the area where the plants were, put on barrow loads of good compost – we have tons of it. Then I want to split all the perennials up and replant say one quarter of each plant and save three quarters.'

Mr Mortimer interrupted. 'But why not put all the plants back so we get a show next year?'

Edmond moved to one side and picked up another of his rolls of paper.

'This is how I see the bottom field from now on, Sir.'

The bottom field was five acres of prime meadow land, flat, and boasting a good foot or even eighteen inches of wonderful top soil. Edmond continued.

'You see, Sir, I reckon we have twenty good varieties of perennial border plants, so I have divided the field up into forty sections of equal size. Each one will be clearly labelled and we can move the surplus plants from the borders into these areas and let them grow on for twelve months – then we can dig them up – sell three quarters and replant one quarter to grow on for next year.'

'But I can't follow forty sections and twenty sections – why make forty available and use only twenty?'

Because, Sir, we have only twenty good species to offer using our own borders as a source of supply.'

Edmond then produced a seed catalogue and continued. 'But from this catalogue I – I mean you, Sir – could buy seeds so we can propagate our own plants and fill the other twenty plots with slightly less well known varieties. We could become well known, in time, as the place to come if you want some of the rarer types of flowers. And we could offer advice as to how to look after the tender plants, or the ones which need lime or peat, and some of the plots could be used to raise rose trees either by planting cuttings or by grafting cuttings on to existing stems.'

'You've lost me there – but I think I have taken in most of what you have said, and I would now like you to leave these drawings with me for a day or two. There is a lot to think over. Oh yes, I meant to ask about propagation – won't you need a greenhouse for that?'

'Yes – you'll see Sir, I have drawn one on one of the sheets of paper and the boiler house to got with it – I reckon it would cost about seven hundred pounds.'

'Oh really – I must look at that drawing in particular.'

It was one of eight Edmond had prepared. 'I'll leave you now Sir – if you don't mind I have my own greenhouse to sort out.'

'Yes – yes of course,' murmured Mr Mortimer as he went through the big rolls of paper again. He said to himself, 'Ah well – there goes Florence's Armstrong Siddeley – we can't do everything.'

Edmond left Mr Mortimer to think about the new plans, and went to collect his bike. He saw Betsy standing beside it – it was Sunday morning and she was in her Sunday best. She looked wonderful. She hoped Edmond would notice. She did not have to wait long.

'My, you look a treat,' Edmond said by way of greeting.

'Thank you, I'm on my way to Church, and I saw your bike propped up there, and I wondered if something was up.'

'No. Everything is all right. I've been talking to Mr Mortimer about extending our range of plants, and he invited me to have breakfast with him.'

'You should come to Church sometimes,' Betsy said. 'It is not old fashioned and stuffy, and they have some good rousing hymns, and we have dances you know, whist drives, days out, picnics too sometimes.' Edmond looked at Betsy and then looked down at his feet.

'Not your sort of thing really, is it?'

'I'm not an old misery you know. Perhaps we could go to the pictures one night. I could tidy up my van, and make it a bit smarter – what do you think?'

'You're on. Any night this next week – any night you like – just say.'

There wasn't a picture they fancied, so they didn't go.

SIXTEEN

Mrs Mortimer saw Edmond leave and she went to see her husband. She was wearing a beautiful dress which was a favourite of Mr Mortimer's. She had taken especial care with her appearance, and was wearing a very subtle, elusive and expensive perfume. She was a very attractive woman and Mr Mortimer, she knew, was a very susceptible man. She wanted a new Armstrong Siddeley car, she knew there was one in stock, in a showroom in Taunton. It was two shades of green, with a leather interior – it was big, ostentatious and she wanted it. She went for the kill.

'Darling I've been thinking about my car and I really must change it. It is ten years old now, pre-war, and quite out of date.' She then noticed the plans which Mr Mortimer was studying, and on each plan was a costing written in red. By way of an answer Mr Mortimer said 'Just look at these plans young Edmond has drawn up, he really is a very surprising boy – he's only seventeen you know.'

'Oh we are opening a shop now are we? Napoleon said that we were a nation of shopkeepers, but I never thought you of all people would want to join their ranks.'

'We all have to make a living somehow, my dear, and pre-war investments were wonderful then – I had over two thousand a year all through the thirties, but two thousand a year now barely keeps us going – this is the way forward for us.'

'Are you going to allow a seventeen year old make all the major decisions in our lives? He only works for us, he's a gardener – a junior gardener to my mind.'

'He is very knowledgeable, and he is merely helping. He is not making any decisions. He is providing me with information, which I have to weigh up. When I have done all the thinking, then I will decide, not Edmond. I will decide what to do next.'

'In the meantime, they might sell that car and I shall be terribly disappointed.'

Mr Mortimer moved from the plans and put his arms around his wife. She had enjoyed a sheltered life; never had to go out to work, always had maids and a cook in the house. Never really had to face up to reality. Perhaps it was too late to expect it now. He reached into his wallet – extracted his cheque book, signed the next cheque and gave it to his wife.

'Is this all I'll need Robert?'

'Yes – don't worry, the garage will know how to fill it out.'

Mr Mortimer's next worry was not cash. He had money enough for all his plans. No, his next worry was how to broach the subject for this massive move forward with the scheme to change Trehaligan into a Nursery and Garden Shop. How to put it across to grown men who had spent time in the Army that the plans for all their futures depended upon the ideas of the teenage boy. It would not be fair for him to claim all the credit, but it would be difficult for Bill and Philip to completely acknowledge that they were working under a seventeen year old boy. Diplomacy would be needed, lies too. The more Mr Mortimer thought about the move he realised that diplomacy and lies were not too far apart from each other. He had once read that a British Ambassador, when asked exactly what his job consisted of replied, 'I go abroad and lie for my country.'

As a first step, he decided he would ring up Major Brassington, invite him round for a meal and tell him exactly what his problem was. Perhaps discussing it would present him with a solution. Mr Mortimer deliberately chose an evening to have the Major for a meal when he knew Florence would be out. That way he could have black pudding and smoked bacon as a starter, steak and kidney pie to follow and then Mrs Bingley's great speciality (forbidden him by his wife) bread and butter pudding made with brandy and cream. He would sort out a couple of bottles of claret. This he reckoned would be his idea of heaven, and he had a strong suspicion that Major Brassington would not too strongly disagree with him. He was correct: the Major did full justice to every course and played his part manfully in emptying the bottles of claret. Stilton was served with the coffee and the brandy, and by that time two gentlemen of late middle age were ready to discuss the serious matter of how to proceed with Mr Mortimer's plans. The Major was shown the plans, and the costings. He was impressed. So much so that he took refuge from the resultant confusion in his mind by agreeing to another brandy. Mr Mortimer also decided that a further glass of brandy might be conducive to clearer thinking, and with a hand no longer quite steady poured himself a wee tot. He noticed as he picked up the glass that the finger or two he had intended to pour was inaccurately showing in the glass. He attributed this to the poor shape of the glass, whereas in fact, he should have blamed a recalcitrant and ill-disciplined hand. Still, having poured it, it seemed a shame to waste it, so he tolerated the slight aberration and felt obliged to drink the handsome double. The Major put his glass back on the table more firmly than a steadier hand would have done. This was construed by the host as a gentle reminder that the glass bore no contents and Mr Mortimer's, by now palsied, hand was pressed into service again. Mr Mortimer then made the entirely unnecessary enquiry as to whether or not Major Brassington liked whisky. The Major replied with as much enthusiasm as courtesy would allow, that he thought he could force one down.

'Not too much mind, we have work to do, looking at the plans.'

'Plans. What plans? I know of no plans,' the confused Mr Mortimer said gaily. Then as if to display a clear mind, 'but what I do know is that there is another bottle of claret not yet consumed.'

'Is the cork off it?' enquired the Major swaying somewhat.

'Yes I took it out this afternoon, so it is at room temperature.'

'Ah well – it would be wasteful not to sample just a smallish glass or two.'

'Want not, waste not, I believe is the old saying, or words to that effect.'

The bottle was emptied by the happy pair, but as often happens in life, the most ecstatic moments are followed by disaster, and Mrs Mortimer returned from her evening of bridge to find her husband and Major Brassington laughing uproariously. It came to a sudden halt as she opened the door.

'It's Lady Macbeth!' Mr Mortimer said. This gave rise to further laughter. Mrs Mortimer closed the door and went in search of one of the two maids. The poor girl was hauled out of bed and told to make up beds in two of the spare bedrooms. This done, she went downstairs and told the two carousers where they were to sleep and with that, uttered some excoriating remark which ended with the words 'you will both be better off in bed, but my bedroom will be locked.'

In the morning, which began somewhat later than usual, both Mr Mortimer and Major Brassington were contrite and subdued. Mrs Mortimer made it known that breakfast would consist of porridge and toast. Both men nodded acceptance of the fact that this 'workhouse' offering was all part of the punishment, only to be expected, and they made no mention of the fact that ham and eggs would have been more to their taste. Mr Mortimer made polite enquiries as to Mrs Mortimer's success at bridge the previous evening, but he was advised that any success or happiness derived from her evening out was expunged by the low behaviour she had been forced to witness in her own home. She left the breakfast room clutching a large handkerchief to her face. This ruse was intended to convince the unhappy pair that tears were flowing. In fact Mrs Mortimer had chosen a large handkerchief to fully disguise the absence of any activity in the lachrymal ducts, but she was content that such treatment was not unknown and must be borne by the weaker sex, and she took a small crumb of comfort from the fact that the Armstrong Siddeley was due to be delivered today, and it would go some small way to making life tolerable for her again.

Once the frugal breakfast was over the two hangovers made their way into Mr Mortimer's study. Mrs Bingley, officious but efficient as ever, had laid out strong coffee in there and just one small brandy each. She looked at them both as she left the room. She made the glance of such a duration that both sinners were bound to look in her direction. They saw a visage devoid of kindness or understanding, in fact the only word which came to mind was 'rebuke'. When Mrs Bingley knew her unwanted, indeed contumacious, opinion had registered, she made her exit.

'Women are curious creatures,' the Major ventured. 'It beats me why some men become bigamists.'

'You don't have to be a bigamist to realise that you have one wife too many,' said Mr Mortimer. 'Come on, let's have a look at your Edmond's work, I want to ask your opinion about how I tackle a few problems I see as regards how the alternative can be implemented.'

Mr Mortimer soon discovered during his conversation with Major Brassington that he was not going to learn much in the way of man-management skills. The Major could see the problem, but he could not see any answers, so Mr Mortimer took him outside into the garden and showed him, in the flesh, what Edmond had put into his drawings and he described how Edmond's ideas would work. The Major nodded his assent to all his guide had to show him, but really he had switched off and Mr Mortimer was left to make his own mind up about how to tackle the problem of human vanity. He decided he would don working clothes and boots and with a spade in his hand oversee the whole procedure, and try as best he could to defer to Bill and Philip as well as to Edmond if any problems arose.

It was September when the work started and he called a meeting one morning and told them how he saw the garden and large areas of the land being used in the future. He asked Philip and Bill to mark out forty plots of land in the bottom field, to make each plot thirty yards long by two yards wide. The business of sorting out the borders, laying all the plants on the tarpaulins and dividing them up he would supervise with Edmond and Betsy helping. The large greenhouse, or at any rate its location, was still a problem, and Mr Mortimer decided to hire a firm of specialists and to take their advice as to the best place for it.

The preparation of the forty plots was undoubtedly the biggest job: the turf had to be removed sod by sod and laid at one side neatly in piles so it would rot down and become a source of compost or top soil for future use. Try as they would Bill and Philip made little headway with the huge task of stripping what amounted to the best part of half an acre. Mr Mortimer kept in close touch with their progress and after the first week, hired two itinerant Irish labourers who worked hard but ate even harder. Mrs Bingley's grumbles were heard for miles. The two men slept on straw in one of the sheds and were presented with breakfast (a pint of sweet tea, and two enormous muffins generously filled with white fat bacon) at about seven o'clock each morning. They insisted that they be paid for their day's work each day as they knocked off at teatime. The money was taken to the nearest pub and slapped on the counter. The landlord was then told to produce cheese and onion sandwiches and beer and to tell them when their money had run out. They kept no tally of it, and staggered back to Mr Mortimer's shed when the landlord said they were spent up. Bright as buttons, they were up first thing in the morning and were hard at it by the time the permanent staff arrived. Two weeks later the forty plots were ready and the plants began to be taken from the borders to their new position. This again required much labour and Michael and Finbar went cheerfully at it. They had heard that a giant greenhouse was to be put up and a boiler house too. Who better to dig the footings and mix the mortar? They could envisage at least another two weeks work before they moved off to Hereford to help gather in the apples and to try to rid that noble county of as much cider as two thirsty labourers could.

Once an area of the established borders had been stripped of all its plants, they were laid out and carefully divided: three quarters of all the good stock was put at one side, separated into small plants, and then wheeled in barrow loads down to the nursery plots. The borders were then dug over, weeded, barrow loads of good compost were brought in, a generous helping of bone-meal added, and only then were the borders replanted – delphiniums at the back, golden rod and red hot pokers in the middle, geum, pinks and low growing perennial geraniums at the front. Mr Mortimer had taken careful note of exactly which kind of plants he had in his borders and he had carefully made permanent wooden labels for each of the new plots, and he spent hours walking to and from the two areas of employment to make sure (with a little help from Edmond) that the plants all went into their correct plots. Finbar and Michael said 'Sure they are all the same to us. If you can't eat 'em why grow 'em,' and they would have planted them anywhere – if at all. But under close supervision all was done properly.

The greenhouse contractors advised Mr Mortimer about the location of his greenhouse and ensured that the surrounding area was suitable for any possible extensions. Also they recommended a boiler with sufficient capacity to accommodate the requirements of possible extensions to the greenhouse in the future, and once they had discussed the whole project with Mr Mortimer they advised him to install a small greenhouse, say twenty feet by thirty feet, especially for propagation. The big greenhouse was ninety by sixty, this was thought to be big enough even for Edmond's and Mr Mortimer's plans. Michael and Finbar did the foundations and mixed all the mortar the builders required, they then told Mr Mortimer they would be on their way. He gave them their day's pay and a little extra for good luck. 'How else would you get to Hereford?' Mr Mortimer added.

'Sure we'll walk it, so we will. That's how we always go, sometimes we get a lift in a lorry, but mostly we just walk it – can we come back next year and help, we can plant potatoes and such like,' Finbar said.

'You're always welcome here,' Mr Mortimer answered, 'but it'll be plants and flowers not spuds. Next Spring we will be busy – do you want our telephone number?'

'We have no use for telephones, Sir.'

'Well take my address then.'

'No. We've neither pencil nor paper. We just remember where to be and when. The seasons tell us, don't they Michael?'

'Well somethin' tells us, and with luck we take notice.'

'Good luck then lads – we'll see you next year.'

'Goodbye, Sir, and you can tell Mrs Bingley from us that her bacon muffins were second to none.'

'I'll tell her – she'll be pleased,' and under his breath he added, 'and pleased she will not have to fry anymore fat bacon till Spring.'

SEVENTEEN

Edmond's plans for Trehaligan were working out very well: the greenhouses were up, and the forty nursery beds were either in use or were prepared for use. Mr Mortimer was amazed at the input Edmond had had, and he sometimes rubbed his eyes and tapped his head and said to himself, 'have I really allowed a boy to change the way I live?'

Certainly Edmond's arrival at Trehaligan acted as a catalyst, but what had really caused the changes at Trehaligan was the passage of time: few stately homes in the country were run in the 1940s as they had been run in the early part of the century. Mr Mortimer's was only a minor stately home, but at one time it could boast seven or eight servants and as many in the gardens and on the land. Mr Mortimer could no longer afford to pay sixteen or twenty wages, and somehow the land surrounding Trehaligan had to be made to produce some cash. Mr Mortimer, now in his late fifties, had worked all his life at his business producing and repairing agricultural machinery. It was fortunate for him that he had been born with a strong work ethic. Certainly his father and his grandfather had never worked, they had lived in comfort all their lives and considered it their God-given right to be so cosseted. Mr Mortimer's years in business had taught him to adapt, and his discussions at his club usually centred around the boy who had transformed his garden. If his friends at the club asked if he was really wise to place quite so much trust in the boy he always said, 'I know a good thing when I see one.'

Edmond's main occupation once the greenhouses were up was to ensure that hundreds, possibly thousands of plants would be ready to sell in the following spring. He also took very seriously the responsibility of ensuring that long term planning would be a major part of making Mr Mortimer's nursery a success. He took to working with Tom Pulkinghorne for most of the week. Tom could not be expected at his age to keep up the pace they had adopted when Michael and Finbar were with them, so Edmond showed him how to root wild briar rose cuttings. This they did by the hundred. These would be used the year after for hybrid tea roses to be grafted onto. He also showed Tom how to take cuttings from camellias, begonias, and grape vines. After a few weeks half the ninety- by sixty-foot greenhouse was full of newly propagated plants and shrubs, all neatly labelled, and each section carried a notice which gave watering instruction: do not water, water every day, only use rain water etc. It was long term but Mr Mortimer was not in for the short-term gain, he wanted his greenhouses and his land to keep him and his workers for the next twenty years.

Mrs Mortimer's satisfaction over the way she had obtained her own way as regards her new car was short lived: she felt the restrictions imposed by the war should now be lifted. The war was finished three years before and she could not see why life should not be as it was during the nineteen thirties. Her life then was a routine of parties, buying dresses and jewellery, continental holidays, and visits to London to see shows and plays. The thought of continental holidays came vividly back to her and brought back happy memories of her honeymoon with Mr Mortimer in Menton, a small French town near the Mediterranean, and just a few miles from the Italian border. She broached the idea of a trip there using the Armstrong Siddeley and staying at hotels on the way down to the south of France. Mr Mortimer said, 'There are strict regulations about how much money one can take abroad, and it would not be enough to finance this sort of a trip.'

'Some of my friends know one or two people in the city and they reckon there are ways around this problem.'

'Yes, expensive and probably illegal ways – if you are found out there would be real trouble.'

'We haven't been abroad for years it would do us both good to have a complete change, or do you think more about your greenhouses than you do of me?'

'Well, it is a difficult time for me just now,' said a resigned Mr Mortimer. 'But if one or two of your friends do want to go, then by all means.'

'Oh that would be marvellous. I'll ring up Dorothy and Alma – I think they will be game for it.'

Two weeks later three intrepid ladies set out with a glad heart and a good supply of illegal currency. Everything went well: the French were glad to see them and were keen to have foreign ladies with a little money to spend. Florence had more than a little money to spend, she found an

English family who owned a little bungalow overlooking the sea. They wanted to return to England and to sell their property in Menton. Florence agreed to initially rent it and then to buy it in two years' time. At this stage she had no idea how she could pay for it, but she had always lived her life this way and was determined to own the little property. The three ladies spent four weeks in France, had a lovely time and reluctantly piled their baggage in Florence's spacious car and set off back to England.

Upon her return, Mr Mortimer wanted to show Florence around his greenhouse and the new plots of land. She went with him and listened as politely as her boredom would allow. She was no expert in choosing the exact moment to impart bad news, and she just blurted it out that she hoped it was all going to be a success because she had agreed to buy a property in the South of France. Mr Mortimer was horrified, 'But we can't afford such extravagance as that!'

'Why not? You can afford monster greenhouses, so why can't I have a small bungalow?'

'But there is no comparison: the greenhouses will help to provide income, and the bungalow will only mean more money going out.'

'Well, I have agreed to rent it for two years and then to buy it. So if your greenhouses are money-makers there should be no trouble paying for it in two years time, and in the meantime we can have lovely holidays there.'

Mr Mortimer was writhing with frustration and indeed indignation; it was so irresponsible of Florence to act in this 'pre-war' fashion. In the 1930s one could take risks of this sort, and he had been at great pains to point out to Florence that those good times were over. He was regretting the purchase of the Armstrong Siddeley now – it had opened the floodgates and Florence had decided from this (ill-advised) generosity, that the financial troubles were over. The proposed walk around the garden and the nursery area was cut short: Mr Mortimer felt in need of a comfortable chair and a cup of tea.

Later that day Mr Mortimer went to bed early, and although he was really worried about his financial situation he was soon asleep. He awoke in the night as he felt a need to go to the bathroom. His left leg would not move and he had no feeling in his left arm. He tried to arouse Florence, but he couldn't speak. Mr Mortimer's knowledge of all medical matters was nil, because he and his wife of nearly forty years had always been well. He prodded Florence with his right hand. She was quick to respond, but not initially as he would have wished. Slowly she took on board the fact that her husband was a very sick man, and she dashed downstairs to telephone the doctor. Mr Mortimer was admitted to hospital, where he stayed for two weeks. He quickly regained his speech and 70-80 per cent of the use of his limbs, but he was told in no uncertain terms by his doctor that he must take things very easy for at least six months.

Everything in the garden went along smoothly. They were all very much aware of and concerned about their employer's illness, but were all surprised when one morning after he had been home from hospital for about two weeks, he sent for Thomas Pulkinghorne. Tom was worried – he had never been sent for in fifty years of employment at Trehaligan. Mr Mortimer received him in his study, where Mrs Bingley was in attendance dispensing coffee and scones. Mrs Mortimer was also there. Tom was asked to sit down and a slightly quavering Mr Mortimer began.

'Tom, I'm not going to be able to take a serious interest in any work for some months, and I do know who is making the decisions out there – it is Edmond – right?'

Tom nodded, and Mr Mortimer continued, 'Philip and Bill might not like this – they are eight or ten years older, and I think they regard him as just a kid.'

Tom nodded again and said, 'He knows more than any of us.'

'My feelings exactly, so I want you, Tom, to act as peacemaker if there are any arguments. I know Edmond won't make them deliberately, but he might *cause* them by making a decision where affects Bill and Philip. Do you see what I am getting at?'

'Philip thinks he knows more than Edmond – but he doesn't, and he thinks he should be in charge now you're . . .' Tom's sentence tailed off.

'. . . out of action,' said Mr Mortimer helpfully. 'Yes, that is how I had reckoned it up. You have a wise head on your shoulders, Tom, and I think you will be able to see trouble coming, and I hope good humour, common sense and a bit of tact will see you through any difficult times. Please tell Edmond, Betsy, Philip and Bill that I am putting up their wages, and of course yours too, Tom, by ten shillings a week starting this week. The arrival of this news should sweeten them all and perhaps head off any little power struggle there may be.'

Major Brassington received the news of Mr Mortimer's illness from Edmond, and he made it his business to visit him twice each week. Gradually Mr Mortimer took the Major into his confidence regarding his overall financial position and the Major, who had always lived simply, offered to lend him two thousand pounds. He could easily afford to do this because his assets had grown steadily since his retirement from the Army. He never took holidays. 'Why would I want a holiday – I've been on holiday every day since I retired,' he used to say. Mr Mortimer promised to pay him ten per cent interest, which was handsomely above the bank rate, and so the Major became a sleeping partner in Edmond's employer's business.

The following Spring was going to be very important to them all, and they all met that most wonderful of seasons with new vigour and enthusiasm. Bill and Philip started by getting the borders and the lawns back into shape, and by pruning and feeding the roses. Tom overhauled the grass mowers, cleaned and oiled the wheelbarrows, tidied up the tool sheds, and did minor repairs to the pigs' quarters and the chicken huts. Edmond introduced Betsy to the delights of sowing seeds. They planted radish (they'll be up in four or five days and be ready in four weeks, Edmond confided). Lettuce and spring onions were planted by the thousand. Also beetroot and, of course, potatoes. Betsy found Edmond's unconcealed delight at the early appearance of the radish amusing. Edmond laughed at it himself, but this only added to his enjoyment – he did not feel at all ridiculous. 'But they are seeds, so of course they will come up – that's their job in life,' Betsy said.

'Yes I know it is, but do you realise that some of the seeds we have sown today are out of the little chest of drawers in the shed, and they are eight years old, and still they are able to come to life. They are just like tiny hard pebbles, but a little moisture and some sun, and the pebble can produce lovely little green leaves – it's a miracle Betsy, just look at the tiny leaves. Surely there's nothing as tender as new leaves of a small plant. Yet they can thrust their way up, and push soil aside to get more sun.'

Betsy smiled. She had been brought up in the country and had seen eighteen Springs, but they had never registered as anything to be remarked upon. Edmond got up from his crouching position where he had been admiring his newly 'hatched' radishes. 'Come and listen to this,' he said, and he led Betsy to an enormous beech tree, near the piggery. 'Put your ear right next to the trunk and you will hear Spring.'

She did as he said. 'What is that sound?'

'That,' Edmond said, 'that is the beech tree coming to life. It is sucking up vast quantities of water via its root system, and by capillary action, the moisture goes up into the branches and the apparently dead twigs start to produce leaves – what you can hear is this vast tree awaking from Winter and announcing that Spring is here.'

The salad season was soon upon them at Trehaligan and they had the stock to meet the demand. The little shop was doing good trade and the sales of plants went up also. The local schools provided hundreds of empty tins, and they were now lined up and filled with pinks, geraniums, lupins, sedum, doronicum, rudbeckia etc, and they were selling. Betsy had noticed during a visit to Taunton market that the fish merchant threw away scores of small kipper boxes. She asked him about them, and he confirmed that he threw away hundreds every week – they were no use to anyone. Betsy asked for a carrier bag full, and though she was not exactly welcome on the bus back to home, she was sure she had made a discovery. She showed her finds to Edmond who agreed that they were ideal for customers who liked plants and kippers. 'But what about the smell?' Edmond asked.

'Leave 'em out in the weather for a few weeks,' Tom said, 'that'll sweeten 'em.'

Mr Mortimer liked the idea of the kipper boxes and he regularly went to Taunton to pick them up from the fish market, and in four or five weeks, the sun and the rain made the kipper boxes a perfectly acceptable way to parcel up plants for the now never ending flow of customers.

Mr Mortimer came to terms with his disability; he had lost ten or fifteen per cent of his physical powers, but he was still active in the business. The part which annoyed him most was the fact that, try as he would, he had to have an hour or two of sleep every afternoon. Betsy liked to, as she put it, 'cash up', at about five o'clock, but there was no one to receive the day's takings and this was a big responsibility for her: there could be fifty, sometimes one hundred pounds in the till, and five o'clock was her going home time. Mrs Mortimer came to the rescue and volunteered to take charge of the money and to go to the bank with it the day after, or as she soon found out, once she became used to the system, she could pop it into the Bank's night safe. Gradually she accepted more responsibility around the business and this led to a more relaxed working week for Mr Mortimer, which was exactly what the doctors had recommended. Major Brassington also became involved at Trehaligan, not just because he had money in the concern, but because Edmond, who was now nineteen, had bought himself a little Morris van, and because the Major had heard that some customers wanted their purchases delivered, he volunteered to perform this service. So Betsy was able to point out to customers, who had bought a wheelbarrow, and some plants, bags of fertilizer and perhaps some vegetables too, that it could all be delivered. Mr Mortimer used to smile as he wandered out of his front door, in his old clothes, and saw the twenty-foot shed which announced by way of a big notice that it was a garden shop. He would see Philip and Bill arriving with wheelbarrows filled with vegetables, eggs and plants to re-stock the shop. His grandmother would not allow a wheelbarrow anywhere near the house after seven a.m. in case the sight of such an unworthy contraption might damage her sensitivities. He would wave and offer a cheery 'good morning' to the conveyors of their ignoble vehicles, indeed he often took his morning coffee out to the shop, just to say 'hello' to the people who had helped him to convert his stately home into a commercial venture. He would pick up a bunch of carrots, or some new potatoes and examine them with pride and say to Betsy, 'I'll bet no one else around here is offering potatoes which are dug up one morning and can be in a pan the same day – oh – the taste of new potatoes with best butter and a little pepper.'

Betsy smiled and agreed. 'Everyone says our eggs are the best they have ever tasted – they have asked if we are going to sell chickens too.'

'What do they mean "sell chickens"?'

'For cookin', Sir.'

'Certainly not – I would hate to rear chickens, make money out of their eggs and then kill them for profit – you tell them Betsy – the answer is No.'

'I'm glad of that, Sir – 'cos I don't know anyone 'ere who could do that job and I'd run a mile if someone told me to kill one.'

'No one will Betsy, you may be sure of that – in fact, I'll wander down that way now and have a look at them.'

Edmond's main activities at Trehaligan depended upon what he was doing, often with Bert, back at his home at The Olde Farm: somehow he felt guilty about experimenting with his propagation ideas and tests at his work place and only felt comfortable taking his new ways of working to Trehaligan once it had proved to be a success. Perhaps at the back of his mind he was still worried about Philip and their age difference.

He knew that seeds were produced by every plant and tree in order to re-produce itself. He also knew that sowing seeds and hoping for results is often not the way forward. The trick is to find out why some seeds are easy to work with and some are difficult, and then once you have discovered which are the tricky ones, you have to take it to the next stage and overcome the problem. Edmond still loved to plant the salad stuff: he loved to see the nutty little radish seeds converted into a tiny living plant in four or five days. He liked to plant lettuce in rows next to rows of beetroot, and take pleasure from the light green contrasted with the red. They are easy, but the ease did nothing to diminish his perennial wonder at the event. To Edmond it was still, ten years after his and Georgina's peas had sprouted, something to be wondered at and something which gave him great satisfaction. He loved to give a tiny seed the opportunity to come into life, and this perhaps is what sums up really happy gardeners: they are the people who have much to give, take pleasure in the giving and have that rare gift; the ability to be deeply grateful about simple things. The constant renewal is an everyday event, but it is still a miracle, but only those close to the soil can appreciate that fact and take irreducible pleasure from it.

Edmond's main success after three years of experimentation and frustration was a nine-inch pot of azalea seedlings. At first they were so small that he thought the pot was covered with some kind of moss. But no, his azalea seeds were through. He made sure the tiny plants received no direct sun. He used only rainwater, and 'misted' them over each day. He tried to ensure there were no draughts, and gradually the seedlings reached the stage where a two-inch pot for each plant was required. He paid a visit to the chemist and bought a pair of tweezers – the kind ladies use to adjust the shape of their eyebrows. He glued small pieces of leather at the end of the tweezers grips, to ensure that he lifted out the tiny azaleas as gently as possible. He then transplanted them into a compost which was mainly leaf-mold and grit and waited to see what would happen. For such tiny plants, they had an amazing will to live and out of over one hundred plantlets, ninety three thrived. They were his first port of call every morning for weeks and after six weeks he took them out of his greenhouse and put them into a cold frame in semi-shade, but where they would benefit from any rainfall. He guessed that in three years' time they would, after transference to four-inch pots, and ultimately to eight-inch, be ready for sale, and then his azalea mollis would spend their long lives giving off that uniquely spiced scent for their fortunate owners, every May.

EIGHTEEN

The daily business at Trehaligan proceeded very well: people got to know where they could, according to the season, buy tomatoes, cauliflowers, salad stuff and bedding plants, and new staff arrived to cope with the extra work. Betsy's sister Sarah decided to join the gardeners and from the seemingly unending supply of siblings, a further sister, Mattie, arrived, thus providing Mrs Bingley with more help and additional reasons for grumbling. 'I've no sooner got one of them lot trained up, and off they goes without so much as a thank you, and I have to feed 'em as well.'

Mrs Mortimer arrived at the Garden Shop each day at about five o'clock with a lockable leather bag provided by the Bank, the takings were put inside, then she would make the necessary entries in the paying-in book and take the bag to the Bank's night safe. She also visited the Bank once or twice each week to obtain small change for the float, and on Fridays, to draw enough money to pay the wages. Major Brassington kept in touch by phone with Mr Mortimer and he made sure that the customers requiring delivery of their purchases were not kept waiting. The routine was rarely disturbed except by the weather and this was by no means frequently. They enjoyed an equable climate and most days, the clement weather allowed everyone to go about their duties, but just occasionally rain would become persistent, and though they tried the age old method of laying empty potato sacks across their shoulders, sometimes it was too much and they would repair to the shed, where, upon a variety of seats, they would clasp mugs of hot tea, get as near to the pot bellied stove as courtesy would allow and then wait for Thomas Pulkinghorne to begin.

'I mind once, before the first war this was, Mr Mortimer's grandma suddenly said to Mr Harris – he was Head Gardener then – I noticed when the men went home last evening that they looked a poor lot – why are they wearing such shoddy clothes? Well Ma'am – says Mr Harris, they are outside workers and it is rough work. He could have said it's because you don't pay 'em so much – but even he couldn't go that far. So he waited for what she was going to say next – it was a bombshell. I want them all dressed alike next week, with collar and ties too – she says. Can't do it ma'am, says Mr Harris, t'aint possible. No one ever said "no" to 'er. So she says, Why not, they get paid don't they? But Mr Harris stuck to his guns and says our kind of work – not that he did so much of it – our kind of work ruins good clothes, and as for collars and ties – them's for bank clerks and not garden workers. By this time she was fumin'. She told Mr Harris that she would have it 'er way, and at that time she had an unmarried sister livin' 'ere and she told 'er to go to an outfitters in Taunton and get them to send up clothes to the house and she would choose what they had to wear. This sister was a timid little thing but off she had to go and after a lot of swapping and changing we all got our new clothes. Course the rules didn't last all that long – the war started and folks 'ad other things to think about besides clothes.'

'I think the sun is coming out,' Betsy said suddenly.

'You're right it is,' agreed Philip. Old Pulkinghorne had just got into his stride and he was reluctant to let his audience go. 'Just a minute,' he said, 'I'll just tell you one more little story about Mr Harris – he had a good garden at his home and he had all the tools. He lent his barrow to a neighbour and about six weeks later this neighbour's little boy returned the barrow and says to Mr Harris, "My dad says he's sorry he broke your barrow, but if you get it mended, he would like to borrow it again."'

So with hearty laughter going out of the shed and the sun's rays coming into it, the gloom of the day was dispelled. Philip and Bill carried on pruning the fruit trees, old Tom decided the petrol lawn mower would benefit from having the sparking plug removed and cleaned. Betsy and Sarah went to replenish the depleted stocks of vegetables and Edmond wandered into the big greenhouse to check on some coleus plants he had germinated, and he was sure the multicoloured leaves would attract the customers who liked house plants. So everyone knew their jobs, and the Trehaligan Garden Shop was busy. The tools were selling well and the turnover was steady all the time, but at the year's end there was not much profit. No loss, all the bills were paid and of course the wages were paid every week, but Mr Mortimer had been a businessman all his life and he knew that a business which stood still was not really going anywhere. He spoke to his wife about these weighty matters over the evening meal and she seemed uneasy and eager to change the subject. This was the normal state of affairs anyway: Florence had never been anxious to admit that they had to resort to 'trade' in order to survive, she was still living in the 1930s when their financial position had been affluent.

The next day Mr Mortimer began his now somewhat faltering trip round his Garden Shop, his storerooms, greenhouses and eventually through the orchard and down to the piggery and the chicken run. He derived pleasure from every port of call and exchanged cheery greetings with all his staff. He was a happy man, and why not. His stroke had not completely debilitated him. True, he sometimes used a walking stick, but he enjoyed looking at his forty nursery beds, his rejuvenated orchard, and his immaculate and now thriving herbaceous borders. He offered up thanks to whoever was listening for the arrival of Edmond, without whom most of the initiatives at Trehaligan would never have been started. He gave credit to Philip and Bill for their steady work and to Betsy and Sarah who were unfailingly cheerful, whether they were in the Shop or crouched down weeding the radish and the spring onions. Tom Pulkinghorne was a great favourite of Mr Mortimer: no one could ever have had a less demanding and more willing employee. He had adapted to working with, and in point of fact, working *under* a boy fifty years his junior. Many men of sixty plus would have been very bitter about such a situation and would have regarded it as a slight. But Tom and Edmond conducted their work together in an atmosphere of affection and mutual respect. Mr Mortimer called into the smaller greenhouse where Edmond was re-potting some tomato plants, and Mr Mortimer noticed he was keeping them quite separate from the vast majority. 'Why is that?' he enquired. 'Why are you keeping those thirty plants away from the rest?'

'You see, Sir, tomato plants will produce a heavy crop for the shop if we feed them regularly and the flavour and colour will be good. But these are for the house (he omitted to say for himself as well) and I feed them more sparingly, and I don't know why, but the flavour is much improved.'

'You would think with more feeding the flavour would be better,' Mr Mortimer suggested.

'Yes I agree, but that is not the case.'

No one argued with Edmond over horticultural matters, least of all Mr Mortimer.

'Well I look forward to examining the evidence as soon as they are ready – I prefer mine fried – almost burnt, and then put on toast.'

With that he left Edmond and walked to the shop. Betsy and Sarah were both on duty. Is there anything more likely to gladden the heart of an elderly man than a welcoming word from two pretty young girls?

'Good morning, ladies.'

'Good morning, Sir,' duetted the two sisters. 'We are sorting out all the tools this morning – during the last three weeks we have sold out of everything and new tools have just arrived.'

'Who took all our stock?'

'Mr Swindells, Sir – you know from the School. Their allotments are very popular with the children, and the new allotments have opened up near the cricket field and they wanted a lot,' Betsy said.

'And don't forget those new Corporation Houses just outside Langport,' Sarah added – full of enthusiasm.

'Oh yes – that's right,' Betsey broke in. ' It seems the Corporation are insisting that the tenants in the new houses have to do their gardens – so they are in here all the time – just look at this Sir,' Betsy went to a drawer near the till, and she took out a child's exercise book. 'Look at this Sir – do you see how the takings shot up at the start of season.'

'I didn't know you had a book,' Mr Mortimer said.

'You don't mind do you, Sir? – I wasn't being nosey. I just wanted to see for my own peace of mind that we were doing all right and that I was doing my bit.'

'Yes of course Betsy – I know you are keen on your work and it shows – you have both played a big part in making this shop a success. I don't know what I would have done without you – may I keep this book for a day or two, so I can trace the progress you have made over the last three or four years?'

'Yes of course Sir – I hope you don't think . . .' The sentence lost impetus as Betsy went in to uncharted territory.

Mr Mortimer gently put his hand on Betsy's shoulder, 'I couldn't think anything bad about you Betsy even if I tried, and the same goes for Sarah – any business which has you for helpers is twice blessed.'

The two girls watched the not altogether disciplined exit by their employer and friend, and both felt very sorry for the loneliness which seemed to have suddenly enveloped him.

Mr Mortimer spent two full days closely examining his Bank statements and Betsy's book. Everything balanced until the time of his illness. From then on there was no balance to be struck. The ever eager and helpful Florence had kept money back for herself and entered false details into the books. She had embezzled hundred of pounds. No wonder profits were down. Everyone at Trehaligan had worked hard to keep the business, the family, the estate, the good name afloat, and the person who held it in least esteem and had contributed least to it, had, by stealth extracted the most from it.

Mr Mortimer took a sheet of foolscap paper from his drawer and carefully listed Betsy's entries from her book and the details from the Bank statements. He found his wife in her sitting room, delicately sipping a gin and tonic and smoking a Churchman's No 1 cigarette. He slid the large sheet of paper onto a side table which was near to her chair and said quietly, 'Read that.' He then left the room, went to Mrs Bingley's kitchen and said, 'I'm going to take a nap, but I'd like you to bring up for me some tea and buttered toast – something wholesome and clean.'

Normally Mrs Bingley would have challenged the word 'clean', but she sensed that Mr Mortimer wasn't quite himself, so she let it pass.

Mrs Mortimer sought to extradite herself from her predicament by taking up the cudgels with her husband later in the day. She began, 'I don't see where the other set of figures has come from, we only get one Bank statement, surely that tells us all we need to know, doesn't it?'

'What we need to know is not how much has been banked, but how much have we taken.'

'Surely the figures would always be the same.'

'Yes – if all the money taken in the shop is banked in its entirety.'

'Are you accusing me of taking money?'

'No – I am not directly accusing you of taking money – I am giving you the opportunity to explain why, for instance,' said Mr Mortimer pointing with his finger at one particular entry, 'on one day last month we took £153 but only £73 was banked.'

'Then you are accusing me?'

'I think you are accusing yourself – £80 is a lot of money – enough to pay all my wages for a full week – and it was not banked.'

'How do you know we actually took that much?' Florence asked.

Mr Mortimer produced the exercise book. It contained a daily list of every penny the shop had ever taken.

'This! This – do you take this as evidence? Prepared by some illiterate shop girl who used to peel potatoes and wash up for us.'

'She had no reason to make the entries except to prove to herself that she was doing a worthwhile job. She had no idea that her book would ever be of actual use to anyone. Otherwise she would not have added little notes in the margins like 'My feet was killing me' or 'Sarah helped me today – very busy.'

'She can't even speak the language properly and you take her word against mine.'

'Betsy knows nothing of this, she has no idea why I asked to borrow her book. I borrowed it, merely out of interest to trace the progress and to look for seasonal trends. It reveals more than I expected.'

The voices were becoming more raised and intemperate by the minute. Mrs Bingley heard what was going on and in a masterstroke of diplomacy opened the lounge door to ask if they would like tea. Mrs Mortimer snapped a succinct, peremptory, and dismissive 'Yes', and Mrs Bingley made, for her, a very rapid exit. She prepared the tea, and since she had great faith in her Victoria sponge she put two slices on to the tray, confident that the brief repast would have a calming effect. At that moment Betsy came into the kitchen, not in her gardening clothes, but beautifully dressed.

'My you look a toff,' cooed Mrs Bingley.

'Yes, it's my day off – I'm going to Taunton, but I have a message for our Mattie.'

'Right – I'll get Mattie for you – she's in the yard. Just take that tray in for Mister and Missus will you – they are in the lounge.'

Betsy picked up the tray and took it to the warring couple. As she entered the noisy room, silence descended with the swiftness of a guillotine. Mrs Mortimer picked up the damning exercise book and hurled it at Betsy. Betsy, a gentle soul, was amazed, and looked to Mr Mortimer for guidance. Mrs Mortimer burst upon poor Betsy with, 'You little sneak – you take our wages, and this is how you repay us. You and all your family, working here, you'd be in the workhouse but for us, and you tell lies and make up slander.' She then rose from her chair and knocked the tray (including the panaceistic Victoria sponge) to the floor – used an indecent word to Betsy, which the recipient was not familiar with, and stormed out of the room.

Mr Mortimer looked at Betsy. His expressive face said everything. Betsy picked up the crockery, cake, cutlery etc and began tidying up. Mr Mortimer put his hand gently upon Betsy's shoulder, and slowly, falteringly left the room. He had aged considerably in the last half hour.

Mrs Mortimer was not present when the evening meal was served. Mr Mortimer was less enthusiastic than usual, and most of Mrs Bingley's excellent offering was pushed at one side. Mr Mortimer lit his pipe, took a sturdy walking stick and went for a walk. He was sure of peace and quiet in his garden. His staff were at home now enjoying their tea. As he walked past the big greenhouse he noticed that Edmond was still in there attending to some horticultural detail, he raised his stick in salutation and Edmond waved back. He continued past the long herbaceous border, through the rose-laden pergola and on to the chickens and the pigs. He had about eight pigs and one of the sows had recently presented him with ten more. He watched them rummaging about in the cabbage and cauliflower leaves – off-cuts from the vegetable gardens. He thought what a blessing it must be to be satisfied by so little in life. They didn't plot and scheme so they could own a bungalow in Menton. He slowly walked back to the house via the walled garden, the most productive area of his property. The whole area of over six thousand square yards was a shining example of fecundity, and he thought about the day Major Brassington had arrived at his house with the young school leaver, Edmond, and the changes the young man had wrought. He continued back towards the house, he went into his study, poured himself a smallish whisky, slouched into a comfortable leather armchair and fell fast asleep. He slept the night in his chair and was awakened by Mrs Bingley's bustling noises in the kitchen. She never did anything quietly, he recalled Tom Pulkinghorne once saying that even her crocheting could wake the dead. He put his head into the kitchen and voiced the opinion that coffee and a bacon sandwich would be welcome. He left the kitchen door open and heard one of the housemaids telling Mrs Bingley that Mrs Mortimer's bed had not been slept in and she was nowhere to be seen. Mr Mortimer settled down with his bacon sandwich and his coffee and thought that she would probably have spent the night with Alma or Dorothy. She did this occasionally when they had had a bit of a tiff. She thought, indeed knew, it would make Mr Mortimer feel guilty. He usually pretended that the faults were all on his side – it brought the altercation to a peaceful end: Florence knew she had been in the right all along and told him so. By these methods peace usually was re-established.

Betsy and Sarah were in the Garden Shop, it was Monday. They had experienced a busy weekend, and usually Betsy had Monday off, but she had decided to come in just for a couple of hours to help re-stock the shop. Many of the basic items like canes, garden string, buckets, brushes, shovels etc had sold out, but there were good stocks of these in the storeroom. Betsy made a mental note of what was required and went for the replacements. She opened the store up, it was always an ill-lit shed and something, she couldn't quite see what, had brushed against her face. She then tripped over a stepladder which was lying right across her path, and fell flat on her face. She turned over onto her back and looked upwards and saw a pair of legs gently turning as on a spit. Betsy screamed. Philip and Bill were passing by and they came into the gloomy shed. They too knocked against whatever was dangling from above and sent it spinning. Bill picked up Betsy who was tangled up with the collapsed stepladder. Philip tried to make sense of what they had collided with. He threw open the big double doors of the shed to reveal Mrs Mortimer hanging from the rafters, slowing gyrating. Her head, at a sickening angle, left no doubt as to her condition. Tom Pulkinghorne heard the noise and came in. Later, when asked about the day's events, he could never explain why, but he took charge. 'Betsy,' he said, 'ring the police now. Do not tell the master – let the police do that – no, don't cut her down, leave that to the police.'

'Why don't we tell the boss?' Philip asked.

'He's had one stroke – this could kill 'im,' Tom said.

Silence greeted this powerful assertion, and they all left the storeroom. Within minutes the police arrived, as did an ambulance. Both strictly speaking could serve no useful purpose: there was no crime, and there was no chance that medical science could prevail. Once the ambulance-men had got Mrs Mortimer's body into their vehicle, the police sergeant – warned as to Mr Mortimer's somewhat delicate condition – went inside the house to tell him the awful news.

Major Brassington at the Old Farm heard the news about Mrs Mortimer from Grizelda, who told him that she was from a 'funny family', definitely aristocratic and very wealthy, but, 'Er brother was strange,' vouchsafed Grizelda. 'He joined the Army in the first War, but they soon had had him out – unreliable, and she was friendly with all them Mitford girls, one of them shot 'erself, and was a friend of Hitler – I always thought Mrs Mortimer was strange, 'ees better off without 'er if you ask me.'

This didn't seem to the Major to be a particularly sympathetic obituary, nor could it offer much comfort to Mr Mortimer. So he got into his car to drive over to Trehaligan to offer what help he could. He found Mr Mortimer looking very old and frail. He took it upon himself to ask Mrs Bingley for coffee with a little rum in it, and a plate of buttered toast. He then went out to the Garden Shop and found Betsy and Sarah. He told them to take a week off work and to tell everyone else on the garden staff to do the same. He then went back into the house to share the coffee and toast and to assure Robert, as he now called him, that he could rely upon him for any help or advice that would be needed.

'You'll hear from the Coroner, the police and so on, refer them all to me, and I'll handle it – I'll tell them you had a stroke last year, and, for now anyway, you're just not up to it.' Mr Mortimer smiled briefly and nodded his acceptance and gratitude.

It was all straightforward: the Coroner had to visit the site with the police, but no foul play was suspected and a very quiet funeral was arranged by the Major. A week or so later Robert rang the Major and asked him to come round for a meal and a chat. After the meal (a Mrs Bingley special of steak and kidney) Robert ushered the Major upstairs to the main bedroom. In there was Florence's desk and the Major was invited to sit down at it, and examine all the papers. It was an untidy mess, but the thing which attracted their attention most was the correspondence regarding the bungalow in Menton. The purchase agreement was extremely informal and from the most recent correspondence it appeared to indicate that the vendors had had second thoughts and were now willing to buy back the property and all furniture.

'It would be very useful to have that amount of money – we do really need another big greenhouse, so I think I will write to them today and agree to their having it back – what do you think?'

The Major knew little of Florence's scheme, but was ready to agree to anything which was likely to add to his friend's peace of mind. All the other papers were Bonds and Shares – presumably these had come to Florence from her family. Weighty sums were mentioned on the papers, this led the Major to say, 'Why don't I take all this lot to your solicitor? He will seek probate and in three months' time you'll be a lot better off and if he's anything like my fella, so will he.'

'Now,' said the Major decisively, 'when did you last have a holiday?'

'Never – never had one for years.'

'Well neither have I – so why don't we go down to, say St Ives, or Penzance in Cornwall and get someone to look after us for ten days or so.'

'What about this place? Mr Mortimer asked.

'It'll run itself – Betsy can look after the money, and tell them old Pulkinghorne is in charge till we get back.'

'Right then. When are we off?'

'Day after tomorrow suit you?'

'Yes, why not.'

'I'll be here day after tomorrow ten o'clock sharp.'

NINETEEN

The work in the garden and the shop continued, Tom Pulkinghorne told everyone he had been put in charge for the next two weeks and his instructions were very simple: 'Betsy, you're in charge of the shop, Philip and Bill carry on with what you normally do, and Edmond and me – we'll just do what we have to do, like we usually do.'

As they separated Philip said to Bill, 'Silly old fool, he couldn't run a booze up in brewery.'

'Well never mind, we'll get paid on Friday so who cares?' Bill answered. Edmond didn't need anyone to tell him what to do: he was in the middle of taking dahlia cuttings. He started the tubers off in a rich peat-based compost in December and by January he was able to take cuttings. He placed the cuttings in the middle of a six-inch pot and these would be ready to sell in the shop by April – with instructions to the customer not to plant out the dahlias until there was no risk of frost. The tubers with one or two shoots left on, Edmond planted into a nine- or ten-inch pot and this he would place wherever there was a gap in the herbaceous border – still in its pot. Betsy and Sarah knew there would be dozens of these prize dahlias flowering from July onwards and they would take them regularly to sell as cut flowers in the shop. The dahlia would be cut down in October – lifted back into the greenhouse and the process would then start all over again.

The florists in Langport and Taunton had started to take an interest in what was happening at Trehaligan, and they placed orders regularly for carnations – the traditional flower for weddings. Edmond was experimenting with the perpetual flowering varieties. Moving into this area of gardening gave him new opportunities for his skills in taking cuttings. Sometimes, if the shop was quiet, he would ask Betsy to join him. So it would be a case of a little demonstration of how to select a suitable cutting.

'Take the strong shoots that still haven't shown signs of producing a flower bud. Leave four or five pairs of leaves on the stem, remove the leaves below that point and put them into a tray of sharp sand. Then they must be kept at about 60 degrees and they will show signs in about two or three weeks. Then we'll divide them up and put them into two and a half or three inch pots.'

Betsy smiled her way through this little lecture. She knew that Edmond was serious about his work. Normally he had a sense of humour and a love of fun like most nineteen-year-olds, but over matters of detail in the garden he was deadly serious. He would say, 'It's the little points that make all the difference. You see Betsy, we are trying to kid dahlias that they are still at home, and home for them is Mexico. Carnations are from Asia and South Africa, so we have to pretend that they are at home too. Where they really are is England with its funny and usually not very warm climate. But we can do it – greenhouses are a wonderful invention.'

'We never did go to the pictures you know. You did say we would, but it never happened – dahlias are fine I love them. But I would like to go to the pictures. I've heard the new place in Taunton is lovely. They have a café there too. So we could go early and have ham and eggs, and then go to the pictures.' This was a long speech for Betsy, and she was laying her cards on the table.

'Right we'll do it next week. See what's on. Name the day and we'll go.' Edmond was quite firm about it.

'I will – you pay for the meal and I'll pay for the pictures.'

'That's very fair,' said Edmond. 'And we will do it.'

They did go, and they did enjoy it – but did it lead anywhere? Betsy thought not.

Mr Mortimer returned from his holiday with Major Brassington, looking pale and drawn, but his ability to smile soon returned as he walked around his property. Naturally the greetings from his staff combined the deferential with the uncertain: how do you talk to someone who has just experienced his wife's betrayal of his plans, followed by her suicide? Most just nodded, smiled, and got on with their work. Betsy said she was glad to see him back and looking so well. The latter portion of the greeting was a lie but some lies are to the originator's credit and surely this one qualified. Edmond took his boss on a tour of the big greenhouse and showed him just how many thousands of little plants would soon be ready for the shop, and then he took him into the little greenhouse and proudly but quietly showed Mr Mortimer hundreds of tiny plants which would in say a year's time be available for sale.

Mr Mortimer patted Edmond's shoulder on his way out of the greenhouse and said, 'You have given me a lot to look forward to, and I am determined to make this shop a major attraction for everybody who likes gardening, and I have a feeling that after all the austerity of the war and the rationing people will see flowers as a way to brighten up their lives.'

One day, at the beginning of the gardening season, a salesman called and asked to see Mr Mortimer. He was selling what he referred to as a hanging basket. Mr Mortimer could not see any use for them at all, but he took the salesman to see Edmond. At that point he brought out some photographs of hanging baskets performing their task during the last season, and Edmond could see that it was filled with blue lobelia, nemesia, and French marigolds. It looked lovely, and as the salesman said, 'They can brighten up a very dull corner.'

'Yes – I can see that,' Edmond said. 'I think we should try twenty or so, and I'll fill them up with compost and suitable little plants, and sell them complete and ready to be hung up.'

'Oh – I hadn't thought of that,' the salesman said. 'I think most outlets just sell the basket and let the customer do it themselves.'

'Selling them complete sounds like a good idea to me,' Mr Mortimer said '– and I'll have fifty.'

Filling the basket with compost was no problem, but retaining the compost was a teaser: old carpet was tried, so was cardboard, but though they might have been acceptable – just about – they did not look like a professional job. The answer was provided two weeks later when Edmond decided it was time to go over the lawns for moss. Huge quantities were raked out, and they were putting it in the wheelbarrows when young Sarah cried – 'This is for the hanging baskets – line the baskets with this!'

'You're right,' Edmond said. 'We'll try it now.'

Of they went to the big greenhouse where the baskets and the baby plants were. Philip and Bill just kept on raking out the moss.

A basket was placed on the bench, moss was put inside it, and spread out to make a lining. Compost was added to the required depth, and then six or eight plants were put in. At this point Mr Mortimer came and saw what his team were doing. 'Just the ticket,' he said. 'They'll sell, no mistake.'

'They will sell better in two or three weeks' time,' Edmond said. 'When they really fill the basket and are budding.'

'Yes you're right – can you fill up all fifty of them – once they are ready we'll hang up four or five outside the shop – then people can see how to use them – I think we have a winner here.'

Four weeks later Mr Mortimer rang for another two hundred baskets, and three weeks later the lot had gone. Edmond decided that from now on making compost would have to be a major priority and the gathering of moss an important annual job. Both were waste products and both could be sold, when they became part of a hanging basket.

The rose cuttings which Edmond had laid out in rows two years ago were now handsome young plants. He had not been entirely confident that rose plants gained by such a crude method were suitable for actual sale, so he had laid out a rose garden. There were now over three hundred roses ready to flower, and they were all neatly labelled and beautifully arranged in beds. The public were invited to see them as part of their visit to the Garden Shop, and enquiries flooded in. Poor Betsy and Sarah were very busy taking names and addresses and telephone numbers. Mr Mortimer got in touch with rose growers all over the country to place bulk orders. He was advised that the best time for planting roses was late Autumn, and they would be supplied bare-rooted – because the rose was dormant at that period of the year. The customer wanted his roses, now, so Mr Mortimer asked Edmond to look into the possibility of selling roses to the eager public – ready potted up, and if this was possible – could roses be sold all the year round? Another problem for Edmond, and he loved problems.

Mr Mortimer had a favourite little café he used to visit regularly when he was in Langport. The owner of the café had a son who was generally thought of in the area as a bit simple. He was harmless, but at school had always been in the special class, and though he was now in his early twenties, he had no job and no prospects. The owner of the café sat with Mr Mortimer one day while he enjoyed his toasted tea-cake and a pot of tea, and since Mr Mortimer by this time was a relatively large employer of staff in the area, he put his problem before him.

'You see, I can't think of anything he could do. He sometimes helps in the café, but he forgets so many things that he is just a liability.'

At this point in the conversation an Ice Cream van's bell was heard and Mr Mortimer had an inspiration. 'Why not fix him up with an ice cream stand at my place – lots of families come now, especially at weekends – it would be an added attraction for my place, a source of income for you, and he would be no longer under your feet.'

The café owner called to his wife, 'Listen love, listen to Mr Mortimer's idea about our Mark – it could work.'

Two weeks later an ice cream stall was in place next to the Garden Shop. What would Florence have thought of that? Or Mr Mortimer's grandmother – who would not countenance having a gardener on view from the house. Fortunately, for the well being of the Garden Shop neither lady's opinion had any bearing upon matters at Trehaligan now – this was the twentieth century and new ideas made money and created jobs.

At the end of the really busy season, the ice cream venture was over, but quietly and with only his architect taken into Mr Mortimer's confidence, planning permission was sought to change the parlour and the main drawing room in Mr Mortimer's house into a café. Mark's father and mother would run it, with Mark to help as required and to run his ice cream stall in the warmer months of the year. From the following Spring a visit to the Garden Shop could include a light meal, or an ice cream, as well as an opportunity to buy plants, trees, shrubs, garden tools and cut flowers. Mr Mortimer was very happy with his little team, his business was making money. He was able to pay Major Brassington the agreed rate of interest on his two thousand pound loan, and though Edmond did not know of it at that time, an even bigger greenhouse was on order to ensure that house plants could form part of the stock in a year's time.

Rubber tree plants came into fashion; everyone wanted one. African violets exploded onto the market in a large variety of colours, and they were easy to propagate and fairly easy to look after. With a careful regime of artificial light and occasional feeding they can be made to flower for ten months of the year. Bi-colours and doubles were available, also fringed varieties, so there was plenty of choice for would-be owners. Edmond used leaf cutting to reproduce plants which were the top favourites and he used seeds also, but found this to be a productive but very slow method. The plant known to millions as the geranium, although it is actually a pelargonium, reproduced very easily via cuttings, and though it is perfectly possible to use this plant in the borders in Summer it was largely regarded as a house plant and almost always gave good value for money.

Edmond then became fascinated by the cactus family. His own interests in this direction coincided exactly with the commercial interests: he wanted the cacti to flower, but his was a disinterested way. That did not alter the fact that the cactus was far more likely to sell if it had buds or flowers on it. He soon realised that they only flower on new growth. This calls for Summer care and in Winter what can best be described as benign neglect. He kept them 'pot bound' and always used Ward and Sankey's clay pots – they were the best and they were an attractive colour, which added to the tactile qualities of the product. He noticed that in the shop, prospective customers liked to pick up a pot and closely examine the little cactus. The fact that it was earthenware and so tiny added to the attractive qualities – the customers wanted to look after, to give a home to, this tiny escapee from the Mexican desert. The Bishop's Cap, he could coax into flower, also the Peanut Cactus, and the Sunset, these he would bring into flower by the score, but perhaps his favourite were the little stones, moonstones, and sugared almond plum, also the lithops varieties, which reminded Edmond of his beloved radish seeds. He always said they were like tiny stones or pebbles, but there was life in them and they could 'perform', to use one of Edmond's favourite words. He loved to present cactus and lithops as a selection in an eight inch pot, and as part of the arrangement he would carefully choose some pebbles which were real pebbles, and then ask the girls in the shop to guess which were plants and which were stones. Only a practised eye could tell.

Edmond's next project was cyclamen. He had seen various colours and sizes, which Mr Mortimer had imported from Holland. He knew that propagation by seeds would be a long job, but he persevered and by planting the seeds in June or July he could have plants ready for sale in fifteen or sixteen months. They were becoming popular Christmas presents, as were poinsettias, and the way people treated them greatly helped his trade: they were usually displayed in a warm living room and though they would flower well in those positions, they would quickly die. But the recipients were usually happy, having enjoyed four or five weeks of good – indeed brilliant – colour. Cyclamen like a cool room, to be kept moist and to be watered by immersing the whole plant pot into six inches of water, so that the water soaks into the compost from below. These instructions were always on the ticket which was displayed with the plant. But most people do not like the person who is receiving the present to know how much (or how little!) has been spent on their present, so the ticket, and the instructions were removed.

The methods of parcelling plants at the point of sale was constantly changing as the years rolled by: the local schools still supplied hundreds of tins, and with holes knocked in they were quite serviceable. Major caterers such as hospitals and large restaurants provided some of the larger tins, and the kipper boxes Betsy has discovered at the fish market still played their part. But industry was aware that there was an opening here for a firm which could be a major supplier to garden shops. People making containers out of fibre did try to satisfy the trade, but the bottoms dropped out of many of their pots because of the damp soil, and though they were supposed to rot down and become part of the soil, many of them didn't, and so the poor plant had no opportunity to spread its roots into the surrounding area. Papier mâché was also tried but with similar results. The clay pot people tried to bring down their prices and many nurseries did buy tens of thousands of genuine flowerpots, but they were still expensive and they did crack.

Then some enterprising salesman arrived with some plastic bags. They were available in three or four sizes, some were perforated, and they were a success in that they were more professional looking than newspaper. But the single biggest benefit to nurserymen during the 1960s and 1970s was the arrival of plastic pots and trays. The manufacturers didn't get all the requirements right at first but they soon made the necessary amendments to the range of sizes and shapes, and just as the improvements arrived, the BBC came up with really interesting gardening programmes on TV. Percy Thrower became the Nation's Head Gardener and at first the nurserymen could not cope with the demand. Garden Centres sprang up all over the country. Some enterprising businessmen had been to America and seen what was happening over there, and they started up similar outlets in the UK. Mr Mortimer's did not start up suddenly and become a Garden Centre: his just grew because by chance he had the right people about him, and because his intuition led him to the idea that people would want to make going to buy plants a pleasant afternoon or morning out. So he catered: the car park grew, the catering facilities expanded, his garden was open to the public and his borders and rose beds became an inspiration to all the aspiring gardeners in the area. They could see the lovely plants in his garden and Edmond made sure that the same plants were available for sale. The orchard was open as well and this resulted in a big demand for fruit trees. The locals could not do all this work without tools, compost, hosepipes, and gardening books. Trehaligan, the one time minor stately home, became Trehaligan Garden Centre, employing over forty full time staff and selling thousands of plants every year.

As the years went by Edmond became more and more the 'back room boy', experimenting with all the, at that time, more obscure aspects of gardening; the sale of plugs (tiny plants), hydroponics, miniaturised fruit trees and so on, but at the same time he was in charge of the staff who tended the thousands of plants in the acres of greenhouses and the scores of nursery beds. This he did because it was his job, but at home on his own three acres he was not a supervisor, nor a scientist, he was just a gardener.

TWENTY

As the years went by Edmond's role as propagator at Trehaligan increased, he acquired Betsy as his assistant, and others to help with the day to day care of the plants once they were brought to life. He had perfected methods of splitting plants, taking root and leaf cuttings, using propagators, raising special ferns from spores and air layering. His love of the moment when he saw a tiny shoot never diminished, and to him the thrill of digging up his own potatoes remained, even though it was now many years since he and Georgina had competed in the Dig for Victory plots at Junior School.

Edmond was now a wealthy man: Major Brassington had died and left Edmond all his property. Edmond, within twelve months of its acquisition, sold The Old Farm – Bert and Grizelda had both retired. He bought a modern, easily run bungalow with three acres of land and spent all of his spare time turning the land into a garden. He spent hours combing through plant catalogues finding rare and beautiful plants which would thrive in the comparatively gentle Somerset climate. He still went to work at Trehaligan but now for four days each week only. This was an era of flexible working hours, so he worked four ten-hour days, and spent Thursday of every week at home, doing his housework. Edmond was forty-five, unmarried but very domesticated. He knew how to cook, work a washing machine – though when asked if he could iron he would say 'what's ironing?' He never went anywhere where ironed clothes would be essential. Garden Shows, visits to other nurseries etc made no such demands, and there was no one in his life saying to him 'Surely you're not going to Chelsea Flower Show like that?' He went just as he was – clean clothes of course – but immaculate? – no, that was never a word, one could use in connection with Edmond's appearance – but passable – yes.

Many people who knew Edmond and Betsy had quietly guessed that they would marry. Betsy, a very handsome and attractive lady now in her forties, had had many admirers. She was as it were 'on view', because she had been around Trehaligan Garden Centre for thirty years. This was a business where hundreds of people called in for one reason or another, every week. So of course she had been asked out by young men, but nothing had developed. Many people who really knew the situation very well, said that she wanted Edmond. He had only to make the first move, but he never did. She spent more time with him at work than with anyone else, and she loved her work: she occupied a special place now at the Garden Centre because she had done every job; she could help in the shop or the Café. She knew almost as much as Edmond about young tender plants, and she was there all the time, willingly, indeed happily doing whatever the exigencies of the day's work demanded.

Betsy's sisters were married by this time – Betsy wasn't. But she was eligible and attractive. She knew one way to a man's heart was via his stomach. One weekend in four Betsy's Mum and Dad went to stay with Mattie, and this was an opportunity for Betsy to try her hand at a Sunday lunch and to invite Edmond. He liked roast leg of pork with plenty of crackling and apple sauce, and this was what he got, but if it was meant as a love potion – it didn't work. Usually – and that word can be used with accuracy because the invites carried on for years – usually Edmond ate so much that he fell asleep after the lunch, and this was not the idea.

Fortunately Betsy loved Edmond at all different levels: she would have given anything to have married him twenty or thirty years before and had a family. She loved him because of his devotion to plants and because of his work ethic and his gentle approach to life. She just loved him and would have loved to share his life completely as his wife. As it was, she had to be content with the fact that Edmond was not the marrying kind, and to have him for a meal now and again, and to drag him to the pictures three or four times a year was as much as she could hope for. Unless something cataclysmic threw them together.

Tom Pulkinghorne was still there, over eighty now, but fit and active, he still looked after the mowers, the barrows and all the tools. He was now the boiler man too. Not that it required any stoking, it was oil fired, but maintenance was important and Tom understood the many controls which kept this powerful boiler on a leash.

Mr Mortimer was still the sole owner of Trehaligan Garden Centre. The indications that he had suffered a stroke grew smaller, and as he proceeded through his eighties no one would ever have guessed that twenty years before he had almost died. He took no active part in any of the Garden Centre's work: but he was still in charge and a benign force behind the progress which was made because of decisions which were usually arrived at during very democratic staff meetings. Philip and Bill were still there, but they no longer experienced any difficulty with accepting that Edmond was the Manager. He never actually had that title bestowed upon him, but everyone knew that the vast majority of Trehaligan Garden Centre takings were as a result of the sale of plants, roses, shrubs, trees as well as fruit and vegetables, and the person who had made all that possible was undeniably Edmond.

Edmond's grasp of how things could be made to happen with plants never reduced his childlike wonder that it did actually happen. He could make really difficult seeds germinate, he knew tricks like putting seeds into the fridge for a few days, or soaking them in warm water. He knew that you had to duplicate the deep forest's ratios of light and dark to create conditions suitable for poinsettias – but where did those dozens of bright red bracts come from? He knew a few tricks but what he didn't know, and he was one of the very few gardeners perspicacious enough to be very aware of this, what he did not know was – how could life be dormant in a tiny seed which was as hard as a stone? Edmond often thought about the seed drawers in the wooden cabinet he had found when he first started work. He deliberately kept back some of the seeds until they were seven, then eight, then nine years out of date and some of them still contained life. Residing in that tiny stone-like seed, year after year, was a determination to live and to reproduce – how had that spark of infinite patience and iron will been placed there? Edmond's constant awareness of this miracle and the fact that he was prepared and indeed delighted to be amazed with every horticultural happening made him the keen gardener that he was. Betsy, as with the majority of people, accepted that a radish seed put in the warm earth would come up – as she once said, 'of course it'll come up – that's what seeds do.' That quiet acceptance was not enough for Edmond. He wanted to know *how* it came up. It was a sense of wonder that Edmond had, whatever is the exact opposite to cynicism, he had in quite disproportionate quantities. It was a capacity to be amazed which children have, and which as they grow older, and they think, wiser, they lose. Edmond never lost it.

His ten hour day meant that he was often quite alone in the gardens and fields surrounding Trehaligan Garden Centre and he would wander into the orchard, say in January, and feel the trunks and branches of the apple trees. 'They are like stone, hard and cold' he would say to himself. Then he would move to the giant beech and oak trees which looked even more incapable of a resurgence of life than the trees in the orchard. 'Will they come to life in Spring – they always have done – for the last hundred years this tree has sprouted – but will it do it again this year?' His thoughts ran into these pessimistic areas – a pessimism born of his great knowledge of the almost insuperable adversities which this huge tree would have to overcome if it was to survive and then thrive: the ground locked solid in ice, the wood of the branches now apparently petrified – can stone give forth tiny tender green shoots? – surely not. Edmond would then go back towards the orchard where each fruit tree had a twelve-foot diameter ring of mulch around it. Edmond gained satisfaction from that – the warm mulch (just like the six inches of leaf mould around the beech tree) was keeping the roots warm – that was where the real action took place, in the roots. The ice would go, warm rain would fall, the roots would arouse themselves, and the process would begin. Edmond would go through these thoughts and his pessimism would then be reduced by the snowdrops. He had spent the last half hour looking up into the branches of great trees, when the evidence he needed was on the ground – the tiny snowdrops were in flower – hundreds of them – a vast burden was lifted from Edmond's shoulders. A spring came into his step – he walked carefully among the snowdrops – they promised Spring was on its way and he didn't want to damage the bringers of such welcome news.

Edmond stayed late one day to make quite sure that the dahlia cuttings were safely making progress. He then walked past the orchards and the nursery beds towards the beech trees and the chicken huts. It was March and it had been one of those deceitful March days which is warm just for an hour or two. Edmond was without a coat or a mac, and the heavens opened. He ran the five or six hundred yards back to his bike – then cycled the three miles to his home in pouring cold rain. He stumbled into his bungalow and tripped over the 'Welcome' mat, he banged his head against the door and fell to the floor, half in and half out of the hall. The rain continued. It was cold, windy and it got colder. Edmond came to and dragged his way into his home and passed out again, with the front door still open. The milkman discovered him at four o'clock the next morning. By five o'clock he was in an intensive care ward of Taunton Hospital, hooked up to a maze of pipes, wires and electrical monitors. He was a very sick man, but he had never been ill in his life and the stamina and resistance he had built up came to his aid. Betsy was a frequent visitor and she was questioned by the Ward Sister as to how he would be looked after once he was out of hospital.

'How long will he need nursing?' Betsy asked.

'Three or four weeks and not back to work in under six weeks,' came the answer. 'Pneumonia can be a killer.'

'Right. I'll move in with him – I've known him for thirty years. He won't like it – but he'll get used to it.'

The Sister smiled and was sure Edmond would be well cared for.

Betsy went back to work and told Mr Mortimer about Edmond's condition, and added that it would be more or less a full time job getting Edmond back on his feet.

'You take as long as you like Betsy, just get him better, that is the main thing.'

Mortality is not a subject that eighty year olds care to dwell on, and in this respect Mr Mortimer was no different from anyone else, but he suddenly realised that he was nearer ninety than eighty and he had made no will. There were no close relatives and he knew exactly in whose favour he should and would leave Trehaligen. He rang up his Solicitor and made an appointment.

TWENTY-ONE

Two weeks in hospital were enough for Edmond to stage at least a partial recovery. He was now ready to convalesce, and Betsy took gentle but firm control of the situation. She had spent some time talking to the Ward Sister and she was determined to pursue a regime calculated to put Edmond on the right track to recovery. She went to see Mr Mortimer and obtained permission to transfer one of his young gardeners to look after Edmond's three acres on a full time basis. She could not run the risk of having Edmond worrying about his precious plants. Then she put him on a plain nutritious diet, every item of which she prepared herself, and it all paid dividends.

After two weeks had elapsed Edmond was well on the way to recovery and he was able to think clearly about the situation: he was a bachelor and under the same roof was a spinster. They were roughly the same age – what *would* people think? He put this to Betsy over a cup of tea and a cheese scone.

'I can tell you what they'll think, but I don't think you'll want to hear it.'

'Try me.'

'They'll say – she's no better than she should be.'

'That's a terrible thing to say – we can't have that.'

Betsy looked at Edmond and said, 'So?'

Edmond looked at Betsy and said, 'We'd best get wed then.'

Betsy burst into floods of tears and said, 'That's the least romantic proposal I've ever heard of, and the most wonderful thing anyone has ever said to me.'

They were married two weeks later. Mr Mortimer sent them away to Torquay for two weeks. He insisted on paying all the bills. The marriage night was somewhat unorthodox, with Betsy making all the running. She woke up next morning for the first time in her life with a man in her bed and thought to herself, as she viewed her sleeping husband, 'Well at least I won't die wondering and neither will he.' She picked up the bedside telephone and rang Room Service.

'I'd like a pot of tea for two, to room 217 please.'

To Betsy's amazement the voice at the other end said 'You can have a full breakfast Madam, if you would like it.'

'Really. A full breakfast in bed?'

'Yes, Madam, everything.'

'Well, I never heard of that – we'll 'ave it – the works.'

'Very good Madam – ten minutes or so and we'll be there, 217 you said?'

'Yes that's right.'

Betsy nudged Edmond, 'Hey wake up – they are bringing breakfast for us.'

'Here – with us still in bed?'

'That's right – this is a proper hotel.'

'It's a slightly *improper* hotel if you ask me,' Edmond joked. 'Anyway you've no nightie on, did you speak to him like that?'

'Course I did. It's only a telephone not a television.'

It was all new to Edmond: two weeks in a hotel, sleeping with a woman, breakfast in bed. What next? As part of his convalescence, it all worked wonders for him. He put weight on, contrary to all the ribald rumours, and Betsy glowed like a woman in love can. They spent most of the two weeks visiting gardens, where else, and went back to Somerset ready for work.

Three weeks later Mr Mortimer died. He was nearly ninety and had spent the years since his stroke and the loss of his wife gently building up his business into one of the biggest garden centres in the country, and as a calm, benign and steadying influence at the centre he was going to be greatly missed. He had asked that his ashes be spread in sea off the Dorset coast at Charmouth near Lyme Regis. Betsy asked if she could be excused this duty, though Edmond wanted her to go with him. 'I do hate boats – always 'ave,' she explained. Edmond said he would go alone and hire a fisherman and his boat for an hour or two, and be back by teatime.

Edmond arrived in Charmouth and hired a boat and its owner for the afternoon. He was no more than a mile from shore and realised he had made a mistake: the boat owner was a drinker; he kept swigging from a bottle, the precise nature of the liquid concealed by a brown paper bag, and Edmond began to feel uneasy.

'Please put that bottle away – you are making me wonder what is going to happen next.'

'You've hired my boat – true enough – but that doesn't give you the right to tell me what to do – it is still my boat.'

'Well, I would prefer it if you concentrated on getting us to Lyme Regis, and have your drink later when we are back in Charmouth.'

How a small boat (this one was barely twenty feet long) is steered is vital to its safety. The boat owner took umbrage at Edmond's remarks and turned the tiller to go directly to Lyme Regis. This meant he was cutting across an ebb tide and at speed. Edmond gripped the side of the boat, it was rearing and tossing, he looked round at the owner and the mad look in his eye reminded of him Robert Newton in the old film of *Treasure Island*. He toyed with the idea of tackling him and taking over the tiller but an extra large wave came and made all the decisions for both of them: they were deposited in the sea, while the boat righted itself and carried on. There were lifebelts and Edmond wore an inflated lifejacket. He made sure the boat owner had a lifebelt and struck out for the shore. He was in the sea for over an hour and barely managed to scramble ashore, where, having rescued himself, he was encumbered with help from lifeguards. He told them his address, how he was officially still recovering from pneumonia and told them to drive him home urgently – he pointed to his car and gave them his keys and his address. The boat owner's brother, no doubt feeling some sort of family guilt, volunteered to drive Edmond home, and this was achieved within the hour.

Betsy was at home to receive her husband, she extracted him from his bundle of blankets and got him into bed. She then rang for the doctor who sounded his chest – looked grim and got on his mobile phone. Within an hour Edmond and Betsy's bedroom was an intensive care ward. The doctor took full responsibility and said it was too cold a day to risk taking him to hospital, so the hospital must come to him. A junior doctor and a nurse were stationed there full time and after two days Edmond began to rally.

One afternoon whilst Edmond was still receiving detailed care, someone rang the doorbell and Betsy answered it. She saw a very tall, dignified man in a morning suit, raising his bowler hat and carrying a pigskin briefcase. He introduced himself by tendering a card which announced that he was Cornelius Latchford, Senior Partner of Latchford and Crombie, Attorneys at Law of Taunton. He was shown to a comfortable chair, he opened his briefcase and extracted a folder containing a document which he handled with the care rarely lavished upon the Magna Carta or the Mappa Mundi.

'Tell me, Mrs Brassington, is Mr Brassington at home?'

'Well yes he is, but he's just recovering from pneumonia and he's not well enough to see anyone just for a week or two.'

'I see. Would it be more convenient if I was to call again in two weeks' time?'

He was so correct in his detailed articulation, one almost expected him to pronounce the apostrophe.

'No. It's all right, just tell me what it's all about and I'll tell 'im.'

He began and Betsy listened.

'I am, or was Mr Mortimer's Solicitor, and I had the privilege of drawing up Mr Mortimer's Will.' He handed a copy to Betsy and continued to drone on about the contents. Which was just as well since Betsy understood not a word of what she was reading.

'So you will see Mrs Brassington that you and Mr Brassington are now the owners of the Trehaligan estate which includes the house, the Garden Centre, the four hundred acres of land and the six farms which are tenanted and pay their rents to the estate.'

'Do you mean Pear Tree Farm, Whistle Farm and all those?'

'Yes – they are part of the Trehaligan Estate.'

'I thought farmers owned their farms.'

'Many do not own the farm, they are merely the tenants of the house, buildings and land.'

'Why is this? – we don't want all this, we have enough,' Betsy said.

'Mr Mortimer's will is quite clear on this point. He specifically asked me to insert the fact that in his opinion Edmond Brassington's knowledge of plants and his hard work saved the estate.'

'Saved it from what?'

'Bankruptcy Mrs Brassington – bankruptcy, and so the Trehaligan Estate is yours – and Mr Brassington's.'

At that point the doctor came into the lounge and said 'We've lost him Mrs Brassington – he just slipped away.'

Betsy ran into the bedroom. One look was enough. Edmond had indeed slipped away. Betsy went back into the living room. The highly discommoded Mr Latchford did not know what to say or do. He gathered up his papers, casting a hopeful eye in the direction of the doctor hoping for some guidance. Betsy picked up her copy of the Will, handed it to the Solicitor and wept – 'I didn't want this – I only want 'im.'

Mr Latchford's day was quite ruined: this was by a long way the most important will his firm had ever handled. Mrs Brassington was now a millionaire four or five times over, he was the bringer of the news but he felt like a cad who had intruded into the worst possible family tragedy. His chauffeur was waiting by the Daimler. He knew when his boss was less than pleased, so he just touched his cap, saw him comfortably settled and drove back to Taunton. There was a drinks cabinet in the rear of the car. Mr Latchford helped himself to a whisky, held up the glass, decided his disappointment warranted a slightly bigger tot, then sat back and dozed his way back to his office. It did not occur to him that the tragedy he had witnessed made his misfortune quite tiny, but he dealt in documents not emotions.

TWENTY-TWO

Cornelius Latchford, however, did have a heart and he was concerned that Trehaligan Garden Centre was now the property of a lady who was not really well versed in running such a large concern. So he rang the firm of Accountants who had always looked after the tax returns, and also the Bank Manager, and he suggested they should all get together with Betsy, who was now Mrs Brassington to all of them, and put her in the way of running such a large firm – they now had forty full-time employees, and in the Summer this would go up as high as sixty.

They met two weeks later, in Mr Latchford's conference room. There was room for them all around the table, tea was served and together they assured Betsy that they were all at her beck and call for any assistance she might need. Betsy found this reassuring, but the next part of the discussion worried her. She discovered that her total possessions were worth over four million pounds. Her total turnover, including the Garden Centre takings and the rents from farms, was over two hundred thousand pounds a year. Her wages bill was about fifteen hundred pounds per week. So promises of help were of course welcome, but mentions of such colossal sums were distressing.

Mr Latchford was sufficiently sensitive to realise that Betsy was having a bad time at this meeting. Everyone wants to be a millionaire, but the responsibility which comes with that happy state of affairs means the happiness can be chimerical. The accountant offered to lend Betsy a member of his staff for say two months, to come in everyday to run the paperwork, until she could advertise for a full time Chief Clerk of her own. Betsy's response was found to be reassuring by everyone there.

'What will that cost Mr Jones?' she asked.

The assembled 'experts' knew they were with someone who already had moved from the position of being someone who needed help at any price, to a future manageress and owner who had her head screwed on.

She continued. 'Does that mean he is loaned to me, and I pay his wages?'

This was not what Mr Jones had hoped for; he was hoping to loan out a good clerk with all the attendant fees, but his reply was what Betsy wanted to hear. Reluctantly he agreed that paying his wages would be fine. Gradually Betsy was acquiring the mantle of owner and manageress, and beginning to enjoy it. The three men around the table were in fact partially beholden to her for a living – she had entered the room thinking these men were in every way her superiors, but half an hour of discussion had led Betsy to the firm conviction that she was in charge of Trehaligan Garden Centre, and this august group of gentlemen as well. She was surprised at the feeling of calm which had descended upon her. She really was the owner of this Garden Centre, the house and the land, and the Armstrong Siddeley car too. She decided to have it sent back to the suppliers in Taunton, have it fully serviced and to use it everyday. She did not want to be an autocratic boss, but she had learnt from the two hour meeting at Mr Latchford's office, that big firms do not run themselves, and she was going to run hers properly. It was decided that the meeting was now over. Offers of help from all three directions were profuse, and, Betsy believed, sincere, but she decided there would invariably be a bill at the end of all the help, and she had taken on board the hard fact that overheads run away with profit.

Betsy declined all attempts to convey her back to Trehaligan – she needed time on her own. She went to the garage which had supplied the Armstrong Siddeley, told them to collect it, and have it valeted and fully serviced, and to lend her a car for a few days until her car was ready to be brought back to her. Word had spread as to exactly who Mrs Brassington was, and a little Morris Minor Traveller was made available for her.

Betsy's home was now the bungalow that Edmond had bought after Major Brassington had died. This was hers too, and the three acres of garden that surrounded it. She went into the bungalow, made a large cup of coffee and took it out into the garden. Edmond had slightly altered some of the levels in the garden with the help of a JCB. He had told her that he wanted to make a raised portion of the garden, put a comfortable seat there, and survey his empire – as he called it. Betsy took her coffee there and looked around. She could see the fish pond full of goldfish and water lilies, kept well back from it was an arc of ornamental trees –

flowering cherries, including Tai-haku, Edmond's favourite, acer brilliantissima, a selection of sorbus – rowan trees to the layman – rubinia and a pink flowering chestnut. Edmond loved trees, but kept them well back from his fishpond, because the leaves dropped in during Autumn and the decaying foliage was not good for the fish. Betsy's eye moved to the long pergola, a copy of one of Lutyens' designs, this had Albertine, Iceberg, Dublin Bay, Compassion (the Queen Mother's favourite) and Mai-gold, adorning it and alternating with clematis, such as President, Nellie Moser, Cote D'Azur, and various of the Alpine family. Edmond loved his dahlia beds and went to great lengths to protect the new shoots from the dreaded slugs and snails – they were up and away now, notably George Howard, a large pale orange flower on shortish stems, Ruby Wedding, Small World, and Zorro and at the back towering delphiniums – Blue Bees, Blue Nile and the pink one, Conspicuous, and Edmond's favourite, Sandpiper, with its white flowers and dark brown centres. Edmond had created all this beauty and he had always insisted that a garden should give off an air of peace, tranquillity and well-being. Betsy experienced all these different feelings as she sat among all this colour and scent. This garden also had a peace and quiet that was disturbed only by the bees going about their business. Betsy especially liked bumble bees, great clumsy insects which looked as though they couldn't possibly fly. The birds were all past their warbling season, but they were there, amongst the plants with good seed heads, especially teazels, and were welcome visitors despite their lack of song. Many plants had been chosen because Edmond knew they would attract birds and insects into the garden.

Betsy sat in the middle of Edmond's garden, something he had created from scratch, then her thoughts turned to Treheligan, another of Edmond's creations. She remembered helping to rescue the walled garden, then the long borders, and the near scorn Philip had poured upon Edmond's ideas about the huge nursery beds – and savoured the thought that those very beds had proved to be one of the greatest financial successes of the whole Garden Centre. This point was raised at one of the 'rainy day' meetings around the pot-bellied stove. Edmond had said, 'I don't care how much money the nursery beds have made, what makes me happy is when I do the deliveries all around the area, I see penstemon, peonies, red hot pokers, delphiniums and roses, and I know most of 'em came from here – that's what we have done – we've turned hundreds of people into gardeners, and with luck their children will be gardeners too.'

At this point among the various thoughts Betsy was enjoying, Mattie and Sarah arrived with their children – they had two each.

'How nice to see you,' Betsy began. 'Come on you lot, we'll see what is in the goodies tin.'

She took the children inside and offered Jaffa cakes and Chocolate fingers. The kettle was soon making hospitable gurglings, and the three sisters were doing what really close families do best – that is, having a good natter and exchanging smiles and genuine warm eye to eye contact.

'When are you comin' back?' Sarah said.

'We all miss you – and the customers do too,' Mattie added.

Two weeks later the owner – the sole owner – of the Trehaligan Garden Centre went into work. Everyone, even Mattie and Sarah, Betsy's two sisters, wondered how things would be. Would everything be different? But no, it was just the same. Betsy took up a stand next to a till and started to 'cash up' for customers. She took her mid morning break and had coffee and toast, just as usual. Bill and Philip sat with her, but the conversation was fractured until Betsy said, 'Do you think those two girls from Horticultural College can take over the propagation areas now – they seem to be very keen?'

'Yes I think they can, but if we run short we'll have to buy in more stock,' Philip said.

Bill added, 'I've heard Ayletts are good for dahlias and Fryers for roses.'

Betsy said, 'Yes I've heard that too, and there's Bygraves and Derby Bros as well. So we'll give the girls a chance, and if we do run short, we'll buy in – they are all doing it now.'

'Don't forget Kelway's for peonies,' Bill said. 'They are at Langport – just round the corner from here.'

'How old are you two now?' Betsy said, right out of the blue. Bill and Philip looked at each other – what on earth did she mean by that?

'I've had someone to see me about pensions, and if you have no arrangements, then something has to be done about it. Poor old Tom Pulkinghorne is still working because he likes it – true enough – but he has only the Government old age pension. I'll talk to you again when I've looked at what is on offer, but this place owes you both a pension – don't worry, it won't be until you want it – I'm going to need your help for years to come.'

Betsy went back to the tills and relieved Mattie, so she could have a break. Two children aged about eight came forward with a selection of seeds and full details of why they wanted them. They confided in Betsy that they had just moved into the area and they were at Pitney Junior School.

'We have a gardening club there,' the little girl said. 'This is my brother and we are both in it aren't we Roly – his name is Roland but we call him Roly – don't we Roly?' Roly nodded.

'I see,' Betsy said and she started to take the children's purchases from the basket, 'Spring onions . . .'

The little girl interrupted, 'My Dad likes them doesn't he Roly?' Roly nodded.

Betsy continued 'Beetroot – yes they are easy – lettuce, carrots, now these French Marigolds are a bit tricky. If I were you I'd have Candytuft or Californian Poppy – they are easier.'

The little girl looked at the packet of French Marigolds and admired the illustration. 'They are nice though aren't they?' she said.

'Listen to the lady,' Roly said, emerging from his silence.

'Alright, I'll change them,' Betsy said. She went to the display and picked out the more straightforward alternatives. The children paid up for their purchases and started to walk towards the exit. The seed packets were in their hands, they were looking at the illustrations and were deep in conversation. They stopped and came back to the counter.

'Roly says he wants to try the French Marigolds, so can we have a packet please?'

'Yes of course you can, but read what it says on the packet – they are tricky,' Betsy said.

The two little gardeners left the shop with their purchases, still deep in conversation. As they went out Mattie came in and said to Betsy,

'Did you see those two – just like little old professors discussing exactly what kind of soil the flowers would like best, I'll bet they become really keen gardeners.'

Betsy then went back to the racks of vegetable seeds and picked out four packs of radish seeds, all different. She ran after the two children and gave them two packets each and offered the advice that 'They'll be up in three or four days – they are like little pebbles but they'll be up – you'll see.'